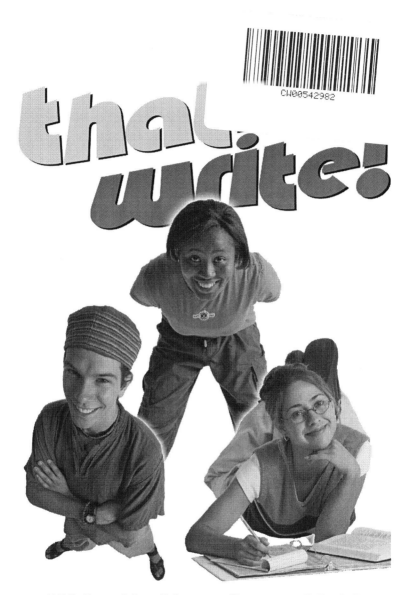

that's write!

Write Up Your Street Vol I
Edited by Kelly Oliver

Disclaimer

Young Writers has maintained every effort
to publish stories that will not cause offence.

Any stories, events or activities relating to individuals
should be read as fictional pieces and not construed
as real-life character portrayal.

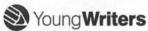 Young**Writers**

First published in Great Britain in 2004 by:
Young Writers
Remus House
Coltsfoot Drive
Peterborough
PE2 9JX
Telephone: 01733 890066
Website: www.youngwriters.co.uk

SB ISBN 1 84460 614 7

Foreword

Young Writers was established in 1991 and has been passionately devoted to the promotion of reading and writing in children and young adults ever since. The quest continues today. *Young Writers* remains as committed to engendering the fostering of burgeoning poetic and literary talent as ever.

This year, *Young Writers* are happy to present a dynamic and entertaining new selection of the best creative writing from a talented and diverse cross section of some of the most accomplished secondary school writers around. Entrants were presented with four inspirational and challenging themes.

'Myths And Legends' gave pupils the opportunity to adapt long-established tales from mythology (whether Greek, Roman, Arthurian or more conventional eg The Loch Ness Monster) to their own style.

'A Day In The Life Of . . .' offered pupils the chance to depict twenty-four hours in the lives of literally anyone they could imagine. A hugely imaginative wealth of entries were received encompassing days in the lives of everyone from the top media celebrities to historical figures like Henry VIII or a typical soldier from the First World War.

Finally 'Short Stories', in contrast, offered no limit other than the author's own imagination while 'Hold The Front Page' provided the ideal opportunity to challenge the entrants' journalistic skills asking them to provide a newspaper or magazine article on any subject of their choice.

That's Write! Write Up Your Street Vol I is ultimately a collection we feel sure you will love, featuring as it does the work of the best young authors writing today. We hope you enjoy the work included and will continue to return to *That's Write! Write Up Your Street Vol I* time and time again in the years to come.

Contents

Tanita Dore   1
Karl Smith (13)   2

Bishop Challoner Catholic Collegiate School, London
Sam Nolan (13)   3
Max Cupit (13)   4
Arron McDonnell   5
Adam Tovey (13)   6
Adem Aziz (13)   7
Warren Gideon (12)   8
Jordan Woodley (12)   9
Leeson McDowell (12)   10
Marcus Richards-Thompson (11)   11
Charlie Wright (12)   12

Corseford School, Kilbarchan
Allan Brown (15)   13
Elaine Clark (16)   14
Craig Gibson (14)   15
Gary Marren (13)   16
Amy Wood (14)   17
Ellie McConnell (15)   18

Cyfarthfa High School (Lower), Merthyr Tydfil
Sophie Ehlers (11)   19
Nicole Abel (12)   20
Jade Saunders (11)   22
Jordan Thomas (12)   23
Sara Jones (12)   24
Rachel Murphy (12)   26
Sophie Jennings (11)   28
Sâra Jones (13)   29
Rachel Phillips (12)   30
Chloe Reynolds (13)   32
Luke Hier (12)   33
Jack Evans (12)   34

Dame Alice Owen's School, Potters Bar

Gareth Jell (11)	35
Matthew Nairne (11)	36
Zoë Johnson (11)	37
Sandy Kiddle (12)	38
Zeynep Livatyali-Esen (12)	39
Tanya John (12)	40
Dionne Findley (12)	41
Daniel Garber (12)	42
Hannah Chapman (12)	43
Chris Chick (11)	44
Mark Whelan (11)	45
Alexandra Maslen (12)	46
Jack Tebbutt (12)	47
Joel Stern (12)	48
Andreas Koulaumas (12)	49
Jenny Welch (12)	50

Newtownhamilton High School, Newry

Louise Henderson (13)	51
Dean Maxwell (13)	52
Simon Knight (13)	53
Kathryn Jones (13)	54

Oaklands RC Secondary School, Waterlooville

Rowan Toomey-Smith (13)	55
Sophie Newnham (13)	56

Roundhay High School, Leeds

Anna Wyatt (12)	57
Hannah Kelly (13)	58

The Barclay School, Stevenage

Keith Organ (15)	59
Justin Feller (14)	60
Richard Curtis (14)	61
Jane Davis (15)	62
Chris Fawcett (12)	63
Steven Chamberlain (12)	64

Steven Slayford (13)   65
James Kirkpatrick (12)   66
Daniel Day (16)   67
Molly Wilson (15)   68
Samantha Foulds (15)   69
Callum Baker (13)   70
Micha O'Neill (13)   72
Liam Boyce (13)   73

The Grove Special School, Berwick-upon-Tweed
Kimberley Smith (15)   74
Shaun Graham (12)   75

Threemilestone School, Truro
Naomi Rawlings (11)   76
Katie Bowen & Chloe Northover (11)   77
Bryony Thomas (11)   78
Sophie Hay (10)   79
Patrick Headland (11)   80

Whitburn CE School, Whitburn
Fiona Cunningham (13)   81
Callum Jones (13)   82
Jonathan Tovey (13)   83
Claire Hutchinson (12)   84
Phillip Tedder (13)   85
Victoria Robson (13)   86
Gavin Catton (13)   87
Emma Dixon (13)   88
Paige Hall (12)   89
Daniel Eisan (11)   90
Blair Adams (12)   91
Lauren Barras (12)   92
Dean Scrimgour (13)   93
Ellis Linney (12)   94
Danielle Ridley (13)   95
Lauren Jackson (13)   96
Becky Nellist (12)   97
Jamie Shotton (13)   98

Nadine Helme (13)	99
Chris Prior (12)	100
Lorna Gibson (12)	101
Matthew Sampson Barnes (12)	102
Ailsa Lilley	103
Sarah Duncan (11)	104
David Shiel (11)	105
Samantha Kerr (12)	106
Kate Shaw (12)	107
Eve Brown (11)	108
Faye Bulley (12)	109
Jamie Anderson (13)	110
Laura Young (13)	111
Scott Bullock (12)	114
Hannah Robson (13)	115
Daniel Bates (13)	116
Stephanie Lee Mart (14)	119
Anna Moutafis (14)	120
Joanne Rossiter (13)	122
Carly Henderson	123
Calum Dobson (13)	124
Kirsty Rodgers (14)	125
Rachael Walsh (14)	126
Rebecca Kranz (14)	127
Amy Edmondson (13)	128
Emma Noble (14)	129
Lucy Walker (13)	130
Imogen Nicholson (13)	131
Harriet Grainger (14)	132
Josh Welsh (14)	134
Sam Harwood (13)	135
Jonathon McCulley (13)	136
Stephen Pollard (13)	137
Michael Booth (13)	138
Jonathon Phinn (12)	139
James Seward (12)	140
Morgan Lowrie (12)	141
Megan Harrison (12)	142
Kathryn Gill (12)	143
Victoria Heselton (12)	144
Jenny Johnston (11)	145

Calum Ross (12) 146
Neil Atkinson (12) 147
Daniel Patterson (12) 148
Jessica Machin (12) 149
Gary Moon (13) 150
Mark Lindsley (13) 151
Emma Jayne Nagouse (13) 152
Eve Calvert (11) 153
Rachael Buckley (11) 154
Alex Rea (11) 155
Anthony Johnson (14) 156
Matthew Hage (14) 157
Craig Young (14) 158
Louie Crake (14) 159
Nikita Young (13) 160
Zoe Ross (13) 161
Daniel Parnaby (13) 162
Matthew Porter (14) 163
Callum Scrimgour (13) 164
Angus Monaghan (14) 165
Jill Croft (12) 166
Frances Richardson (12) 167
Anna Robinson (11) 168
Michael Scott (12) 169
Jade Pape (11) 170
Jack Routledge (12) 171
Rae Lindstaedt (12) 172
Katy Sutcliffe (16) 173
Jake Campbell (15) 174
Elizabeth Plumpton (15) 175
Philip Vasey (16) 176
Miriam Phipps Bertram (16) 177
Kay Parmley (11) 178
Alexander Wood (11) 179
Laura Dixon (12) 180
Alice Urwin (12) 181
Anthony Jeffries (11) 182
Lindsey Miller (13) 183
Aaron Porter (16) 184
Lee Forster (16) 185
Owain Curtis (13) 186

David Blenkinsop (13) 187
Christopher Ovington (11) 188
Siobhan Tedder (11) 189
Joel Middleton (12) 190
Sam Prior (11) 191

The Creative Writing

Alice

Mary pulled out some of the pictures of her husband John from under her dusty bed. She often did this, as it reminded her of the happier times when her husband was alive. John tragically passed away during war a year ago to this day, leaving his wife and two children, Molly and Darren. Molly came in.

'It's been a year, hasn't it Mum?' she said.

Mary nodded. Mary's fine hair swept across her pale face as she tried to hold back the tears. Darren came in too.

The three of them sat around the table and Mary held her box of John's belongings under her arm. She just stared. It was the memories all over again. She couldn't block out the secret that her and John had kept from the children since they were born. It seemed much easier to hide when John was alive, much easier. She began to feel uneasy, but the sight of the children - she couldn't bear to upset - who were laughing and joking over what their dad used to be like, warmed her heart, but she could not live with this guilt anymore. The remorse hanging over her, she decided to tell it. The words were on the edge of her tongue, ready to spill, when all she could say was, 'Kids.' They looked up and she burst into tears. 'I'm so sorry, really sorry, please forgive me,' she sobbed. She pulled out a picture of a baby. 'This is your sister Alice,' she said.

Tanita Dore

The Secret Gerbil

It stood on its hind legs looking at me. It was this little brown thing with two beady eyes and no bigger than a ping-pong ball. It stared, I stared back. Then it gave up and went back to chewing. Then it gave up and went back to chewing. Then I noticed what Tiny, my gerbil, was chewing. It was a square piece of steel curved at the edges. I opened the door to Tiny's cage and grabbed it. I went through this icy barrier and all of a sudden I was Tiny.

Where am I? How did I get here? Question after question running through my head. The very last question - *how do I get out of this; clown-footed, long tailed, small-handed body?* I knew the answer, The Silver Square!

I knew how to escape, get the barred door on the side of the cage open. I thought long and hard. Then it hit me. I went up the barred stairs to the top of the cage where Tiny's pine house was. I pushed and pushed until it went off the side and plunged into the door opening. I was free.

I touched the silver thing. I felt funny all over, then suddenly I woke up. My gerbil was staring at me again. *Just a dream,* I thought, as I got up walking to the bathroom, my tail trailing behind.

Karl Smith (13)

Joy Riding

Steve and Terry were two 15-year-olds that were always getting into trouble at school. They constantly had fights with other kids in the school.

One Tuesday evening on their way out of another hour detention they noticed as their head teacher got back out of her car to get something she had left the car open with the engine running.

'Let's take it,' said Steve.

'Yeah. They won't like that,' replied Terry. They ran over to the car and Steve got in the driver's seat and sped off.

Just after they got round the corner the head teacher came out of the school, looked at where her car should have been and stood there bemused. She ran back in and phoned the police.

Steve and Terry were now driving as fast as possible down a motorway when they noticed a blue flashing light coming up behind them. They had forgotten about the police.

They had been driving now for 2 hours and the police had constantly followed them when they were shunted. They almost swerved off the road. The second shunt came and they flew off the road, flipped over and the car landed on its roof. No one was moving. A policeman walked up to them and they were both crushed. They were *dead* . . .

Sam Nolan (13)
Bishop Challoner Catholic Collegiate School, London

Bad News For Football Hooligans

Ex-Arsenal goalkeeper David Seaman backs up the hooligan hotlines as he said, 'This country has a terrific football reputation which is damaged by only a small percentage of people who act like yobs and cause trouble.'

If the hooligans start causing trouble in Portugal the England team may be thrown out of Euro 2004.

If you have any information on football yobs call us on 0207 527 52 53 or on 0800 592 16 32.

Max Cupit (13)
Bishop Challoner Catholic Collegiate School, London

We're Scared Of No One

The mood in the England camp is low after they are told John Terry will not play against France. The England centre back has only been declared 70 per cent fit as he has hamstring problems. Even though Terry will take no part in the match he has claimed, 'We're scared of no one and will go into this match full of confidence with or without me'. Possible replacements for the centre position is likely to be Jamie Carragher or Ledly King. Sol Campbell, Terry's partner also stated, 'France are the team under pressure to retain their title not us and we are going into the game not to hold them off for a draw but to go on for a big victory'.

Arron McDonnell
Bishop Challoner Catholic Collegiate School, London

Young Writers – That's Write! Write Up Your Street Vol I

5

Stars

Over one thousand years ago, the planet Earth was at its best. The trees were bright green, the flowers bloomed with pride and the animals hopped merrily. But all of this was about to change. In a dark volcano, the dark Lord Ruire made another type of animal, but these animals were pure evil . . .

Stars

These animals were called men. These men stood up on two legs and they made the axe and spear. One by one, the animals were being killed, so the Lord of the animals, Sappby, declared war against men.

On Friday 13th the war broke out. Ruire called his men to attack, Sappby called his animals to attack. Both sides hit each other with a mighty clash. Suddenly, Sappby stopped, he looked down, sticking out of his chest, was a human spear. Sappby fell on the floor, and died. And as his body hit the ground, his soul rose from his body. His soul had turned into a star. And every animal that died after that, their soul would turn into a star too.

But sadly, the humans won the war, so from that day on, at night, the stars would shine brightly, so that everyone will remember the great battle that took place, on Friday 13th.

Adam Tovey (13)
Bishop Challoner Catholic Collegiate School, London

A Day In The Life Of A Pen

Click, click, click, click . . .

I wish he would stop doing that, it's not just annoying me the whole class hate it to.

Click, click, click, click.

'Mark, will you please stop making that noise,' said the teacher. Mark stopped.

That's better I can't hear myself think with that noise, oh yes before I forget I'm Paul the Pen and that was me moaning about the click sound, it's just Mark mucking about with my lid, up and down and up and down, it gives me an ink ache.

Anyway I'm here to tell you about the life of a pen and despite what you might think it's very hard, we don't just lie in a pencil case all day we have a very difficult life, take yesterday for example. I was jammed in that pencil case with loads of other pens, there was hardly enough room to breathe. I was finally taken out at first period where I had to write loads of stuff about algebra a to the power of 2 or something, it's all mumbo jumbo to me anyway.

When the lesson was over I was stuffed in the pencil case and strangely not taken out till third period (I later found out that period 2 was a reading lesson) which was a double lesson on science in which I got dropped in acid, stepped on and thrown across the room (they had a supply teacher). But finally, oh joy, periods 5 and 6 came and it was PE so I got to rest.

When we got home there was another reason to celebrate, he had no homework so I got an extended rest. You know what, in retrospect my life isn't so bad, it could be worse, I could be a rubber.

Adem Aziz (13)
Bishop Challoner Catholic Collegiate School, London

Quick Defeat

England 1 - France 2

England got off to a flying start by Frank Lampard's beautiful header on the 37th minute, *but* it all went downhill as in injury time in the second half, due to Emile Heskey's terrible challenge on Zidane. Zidane took a free kick just out of the box, he delivered the ball into the top left hand corner.

Gerrard's pass back gave France's Thierry Henry a great advantage, but David James trying to be the hero, took Henry's legs and gave France a penalty, Zidane made no mistake but to put the ball away for good.

The commentator's words were, 'Who's going to be the hero, Zidane or James?' But sadly it was Zidane.

England's captain, David Beckham was stewing because of missing his penalty as Barthez saves it.

But don't worry England are not out yet, let's hope they beat Switzerland.

Warren Gideon (12)
Bishop Challoner Catholic Collegiate School, London

The Sun

The goldfish monotor, the Loch Ness Monster has turned out to be the smallest, tiniest goldfish in the whole world. It even has been used as a scientific experiment. Scientists think this could be used in some sort of food during the season of evolution.

Jordan Woodley (12)
Bishop Challoner Catholic Collegiate School, London

The Dog Thief

Yesterday, the third dog was stolen in East London's Hackney in the middle of the night when a white lady was walking her dog at 9 o'clock at night. She was seen by an eyewitness who said, 'I was just smoking outside my window when I saw these three black youths walk up to the old lady from behind and steal her dog'.

The eyewitness said that the boys were wearing black *Avirex* jackets and black Nike trainers which fits the day before's statement coming from a passer-by who saw another white lady get attacked and was seriously injured and put in hospital. If these boys are seen please call crime numbers 0207 8263651 or the police on 999.

Leeson McDowell (12)
Bishop Challoner Catholic Collegiate School, London

A Day In The Life Of Zidane

When we were playing England yesterday when England was winning 1-0 I thought they'd won the match because it was going into the 90th minute, but when Makele won the free-kick I thought, *yes we might have a chance of drawing.* It was down to me or Henry, but Henry said, 'You take it.' So I stepped up to the ball, I was thinking, *where should I place it?* The ref blew the whistle, I ran and looked up and I shot. It went over the wall and it went in the back of the net. I was thinking, *yes, we've drawn,* but suddenly we kicked off and we just booted it up there. The England team was playing good one-twos, then Steven Gerrard kicked the ball back to James but Henry had the ball, he left the defenders and tried to take it round James but James caught Henry on his leg, it was a penalty, I was taking it. If I scored I'd win for France. I kicked the ball, it went to the bottom corner, we won, the match ended 2-1 to France.

Marcus Richards-Thompson (11)
Bishop Challoner Catholic Collegiate School, London

A Day In The Life Of A Book

What do they take me for, a trash site? I'm sick of this drawing and graffiti on me like those hooligans out there. My spine is going to rip, tearing until my flesh comes away from me.

There is a smell all around me and it smells like sweaty rotten eggs. I'm aching all over and I can't move away from this unpleasant smell unless someone moves me again.

Bang. Bang. Bang. It's like a stampede coming for me but it's them again, they are like giants to me, I can barely see their faces. I'm always falling on the floor. Ouch, here I go again. What is the matter with their brains? You can't get anything through to them.

When theygo to sleep, I am grateful that sleeping came into the world.

Charlie Wright (12)
Bishop Challoner Catholic Collegiate School, London

A Night At The Horse Riding

My name is Autumn. I am big and brown in colour. I live in a stable and eat hay, horse food and drink water. I am quite lazy, I like to take my time going round the indoor arena. I have got used to people walking beside me because there are three people walking beside me, one leading me and one either side of me in case my rider leans to one side. We play games in teams and we also do obstacle courses. There are four people in the group, 2 girls and 2 boys. Some weeks we do a little bit of trotting. My rider is on me for an hour from 7 o'clock until 8 o'clock. I have the same rider every week, unless they are not well. Sometimes there are not enough helpers for all the riders to go on at the same time so they have to split them into half and hour each, but it doesn't happen often.

I think my rider enjoys coming riding because he enjoys talking to his side walkers. He plays games, while on my back. We look for cuddly toys the instructor has hidden around the arena. When I finish my night's work I look forward to a treat, a big red juicy apple!

Allan Brown (15)
Corseford School, Kilbarchan

A Day In The Life Of James Lang

James was my mum's dad. He was my grandpa. I really miss him. He died on the 8th of October 2001 and he was 70 years of age.

He lived on a farm until he became really ill and was unable to go outside and work. Then he used to sit in a chair and look out of the window at his farm.

My grandpa got up at seven o'clock in the morning to start his day. His first job would be to feed all of the animals. He looked after sheep, cows, lambs and some bulls. He sometimes called the bulls Big Johnny Bulls. When he was finished feeding all of the animals, he would go back home. Granny would make him a big plate of porridge. He liked his porridge in the morning, very much.

After his porridge he went back outside and drove a tractor in the fields. He used to wear a pair of blue dungarees on top of his own clothes, to keep them clean.

After he'd had his lunch he used to go through to the living room and have a sleep. Then in the afternoon he went back outside to the fields, to finish his working day off. He would do this every day. He never moaned because he had to get up early in the morning, he liked to get up early in the mornings.

Everybody misses him.

Elaine Clark (16)
Corseford School, Kilbarchan

My Rabbits

I have two rabbits, their names are Thumper and Kia. Thumper is fat, grey and has two big ears. Kia is thin and white. They live outside in huts. They drink water, they eat rabbit food and grass.

In the morning they have a drink. Thumper lies in his hut all day. He is very lazy. Sometimes he runs around the garden. Thumper does not like to go back in his hut. Kia runs round her hut all day. She likes running in the garden too.

When Thumper is in my home he lies under the heater. I give them their dinner at night. Then Thumper goes to sleep again. Kia does not go to sleep, she likes to run. My rabbits are very happy.

Craig Gibson (14)
Corseford School, Kilbarchan

Ben

I am a dog called Ben. I am black all over. I am big and fat. I am 5 years old with big, long, floppy ears. I am a cross between a Labrador and a spaniel. I wear a red collar with my name on it. When I hear somebody moving about upstairs I bark. When the family come down the stairs in the morning I am happy to see them.

I go for a walk in the morning with Gary's cousin. He lets me off the lead to run about. He plays with me all day until Gary comes home from school. I like to drink milk and have a big tin of dog food at half past 5. We wait for a while to let my dinner go down.

I go for a walk with my cousin John and Gary after school. I like going for a walk with my brother, who stays next door. When we go out together we like to run about with a ball and some sticks.

There is a cat in the house too and we get on well together. When the cat had kittens I went to see them but she chased me away because she was protecting her kittens. I was upset.

If anybody is going past my house and if the window is open I jump out the window and bark at people because I have to look after my family. When everyone goes to bed I have to listen out, to take care of everyone. I really like my days.

Gary Marren (13)
Corseford School, Kilbarchan

Amy's Day Out

One Sunday Amy went for a walk in the park with Mum, Dad and brothers Neal and John. Some of her friends from school went with her too, they were Elaine, Ellie, Louise, Lauren and Jenna. Lauren was in her power drive. The park was very busy.

At the beginning of their walk it was nice and warm but after a while it began to get very cold. Amy was excited because she thought it might snow. Her mum was worried because no one had taken a hat, scarf or gloves with them.

Everyone decided to go back to Amy's house. When they got there, Amy's mum went into the kitchen to make something nice for everyone to eat, they all had a cup of hot chocolate to warm themselves up.

Walking in the park had tired them all out so they settled down to watch a Harry Potter video. Everyone was very happy, especially Amy.

Amy Wood (14)
Corseford School, Kilbarchan

A Day In The Life Of Bruce

I am called Bruce, I am about 4 years of age. I have a very soft coat. I do not like getting brushed very much. I like going for walks with my dad. When I go out my dad takes me down to the water and I jump straight in, but when I get home I have to stay in the kitchen until I am dry. When I am allowed out of the kitchen I have a mad five minutes by bringing out all my toys from under the breakfast bar. My mum goes off her head when I do this, so I go into my box and sleep.

I can smell something nice, it is time for my dinner. This is my favourite time of the day.

After my dinner I sometimes like to lay up on top of Ellie's bed with her. I think Ellie likes it when I put my head under her arm. One of the games I love to play is football with my brother Tom. Something that I do is grab my tail and go round in circles. I have been at Ellie's house since I was 6 weeks old because my mum wasn't able to give me milk any longer. I love it when my boss takes me to my dog training to see my dog mates.

I am a very happy dog all round.

Ellie McConnell (15)
Corseford School, Kilbarchan

The Beauty Within

Once long ago, when the world was young, in the heavens of the Greek gods, there lived a beautiful princess named Beauticia. She was very vain, she spent all her time admiring her beauty. Beauticia had no time to be nice or caring to anyone, not her family or friends, only herself and her beauty. People around her often needed help or kindness from her but she neglected everything except her looks.

Beauticia was so vain that one day she decided that she would have her whole room decorated with mirrors so that she could admire herself wherever she looked. She had mirrors installed on her walls, her floor and her ceiling. Beauticia's vanity was to be her downfall.

One fateful day, the mighty Zeus, king of the gods, was displeased by his people and got very angry. His voice thundered and his fists slammed, all this violent release of his anger caused the heavens to shake and shake, like a huge earthquake. Beauticia was in her room as all the mirrors started to crack and break and fall over her, cutting and scarring her beautiful face, arms, shoulders, hands and legs.

After some time Beauticia's cuts healed, although some were very deep, but she was left with hideous scarring all over her face and body, she had lost her beauty, she was in fact ugly.

Beauticia was very sad and ashamed to be seen, and never wanted to see herself in a mirror, she became lonely.

People around Beauticia were sorry for her, they were kind and friendly and helpful, she was sorry that she had not been kind to them in the past.

Over time Beauticia changed, she became kind and caring and thoughtful, and people forgot about her scars and ugliness, to them she was beautiful on the inside, where it counts.

Sophie Ehlers (11)
Cyfarthfa High School (Lower), Merthyr Tydfil

Young Writers – That's Write! Write Up Your Street Vol I

19

Spartacus And The Golden Wings Of Apollo

King Neptune had put all the people of Thebes in prison for trying to overrule him. Spartacus, the town's hero, had narrowly escaped prison because he had been visiting Hercules on Mount Olympus. When he had come back from Mount Olympus and found he was the only person left in Thebes, he went to visit King Neptune at the royal palace.

'What has happened to the people of Thebes?' exclaimed Spartacus.

'They are all in prison,' said King Neptune, an evil smile spreading across his face, 'for trying to overrule me!'

'You've got to set them free or you will have to answer to me!' shouted Spartacus angrily.

'I will not fight you Spartacus, I've warriors for that, but I will set you a challenge,' stated King Neptune stroking the beard on his chin. 'If you can get me The Golden Wings of Apollo I will set the people of Thebes free.'

'I'll do it,' replied Spartacus who promptly marched out of the palace; he would now set out for The Glades of Saturn.

The next day he arrived at The Glades of Saturn early in the morning when the sun was low in the sky, the sun was a fiery orange and the sky a pale pink. He now needed to find The Golden Wings of Apollo. He looked across the green meadows and noticed a golden glow. He raced across the grass, he jumped over flowers and leaped over bushes. Soon he had arrived at a huge maze, he looked across to the golden glow; *this is where The Golden Wings must be,* he thought. He crept into the maze. For as far as he could see there were towering mint-green hedges with rosy red, snow-white, sunshine-yellow and plum-purple roses sticking out of it. He turned to the right; he quickly walked along the yellow bricked path. He turned to the right, then a sharp left and walked into a half lion, half eagle. A Gryphon. Its bottom half was covered in mud-brown and stony grey feathers with paws that had sharp claws, so sharp that they looked like gleaming knives. Its top half was covered with a mellow yellow fur, along its neck it had a mane of hair that was a shining orange, its teeth could chew a human easily and its eyes had a menacing look about them as if daring anyone to pass him.

'You are on the right path to The Golden Wings of Apollo,' roared the Gryphon. 'If you answer my riddle correctly you can pass through without me harming you, if you answer my riddle wrongly I will harm you. But if you choose not to have a go at my riddle I will also harm you. What is your choice?'

'I will solve your riddle. What is it?' Spartacus asked.

'Here is the riddle . . . I run but I have no legs. What am I?' questioned the Gryphon.

'What runs but has no legs?' Spartacus said to himself. 'I've got it . . . it's a nose,' he said.

The Gryphon leapt aside to leave the way clear. Spartacus hurried along the narrow path. It was getting lighter. He took a left and he saw it - The Golden Wings of Apollo. They were sitting on a creamy pedestal. They were as fluffy as a cloud and as gold as an eagle's eye, and shining as bright as the sun on a hot summer's day. Spartacus walked slowly to them, he slipped them on, he started to rise steadily off the ground up, up and up, soon he was as high as the clouds.

When he arrived back in Thebes he went straight to the royal palace to see King Neptune.

'You have stuck to your challenge so I will stick to my promise. Set the people free,' shouted the King to his servants.

Later that day Spartacus was carried in triumph by the grateful crowd through the streets of Thebes, feeling as if he had conquered the world with a smile that spread from ear to ear.

Nicole Abel (12)
Cyfarthfa High School (Lower), Merthyr Tydfil

Butch The Saviour

The thin warmth of the winter sun had begun to disappear. The ground turned from its beautiful green grass and flowers to a silvery icing of frost. A dog stood by the great wooden door and breathed in the cold, sharp air, it was as sharp as knives slicing at your tongue.

Butch was a great hunting dog. Butch was the bravest and most intelligent of them all. Butch could run swiftly and only Butch could catch birds and foxes as skilfully.

'Butch!' Caradog was calling him.

Butch felt a shiver run up and down his spine. He felt very uneasy.

'Come on Butch!' he demanded. 'We're going hunting!'

With that Butch ran to the prince and set off to hunt.

One dull, grey evening Butch felt as if something was worrying him. Was it some kind of animal? Siwan, Caradog's wife, came out with her baby son. He came out to watch his father go off hunting. Then when he had gone, the baby spotted Butch sitting in the corner.

'It's time for the baby's nap!' shouted the housemaid. She put him in his cradle.

Butch stood outside the chamber. The maid went to prepare supper for the prince and his hunters. Butch closed his eyes.

Suddenly, they sprang open, a sudden movement, he pushed the door open and there was a figure standing in the doorway, *a wolf!*

The battle was very fierce. The wolf bit Butch's ear but Butch managed to escape the wolf. Butch's teeth sank into the wolf's neck and the wolf dropped dead, the cradle was upside down and Butch was covered in blood.

Caradog came back and saw the bloodstains on the floor. 'You have killed my son!' shouted Caradog. And without another word he drew his sword and struck it right into Butch. The cry of the baby echoed through the prince's ears. Sivan got the baby.

'A wolf!' cried the nursemaid.

Poor old Butch, he saved the baby and killed a wolf, but he had also been killed.

Jade Saunders (11)
Cyfarthfa High School (Lower), Merthyr Tydfil

The Midas Touch

The true story of King Midas; it all started at a rock 'n' roll competition when King Midas chose a woman to win that was tone deaf, just because she was very pretty. The young talented man that should have won was very angry and turned King Midas' ears into elephant ears. This was kept a secret and no one knew except when he had his hair cut by a barber, he saw them and laughed, but he promised not to tell anyone. When the barber went out he just laughed for no reason and people were getting very curious, but he never told anyone as he did not want to be punished by the king.

On the way home King Midas came across a beast that was a Minotaur, tattooed on his back was a list of all the bad things that had happened in Pandora's box. He granted the king a wish, any wish, he could have got rid of his ears but being as greedy as he is, he wished that everything he touched turned to gold.

When he got home he went in his garden and as he walked everything he touched turned to gold; trees, a bench, grass, the fish in the pond.

When he was having his Chinese he touched a noodle and it turned to gold as he was putting it in his mouth. 'Argh! I have broken my tooth.'

When his son came running in he had his walkman on and did not hear his father shouting, 'Don't touch me,' but it was too late, as he put his arms around him and he turned to gold. Because his son turned to gold, he screamed and shouted that he wished that everything was back to normal.

The Minotaur said, 'If you want to get rid of the wish go and bathe in the river,' so he did and everything went back to normal. But to this day you can still hear the river weeds whispering that King Midas has elephant ears.

The lesson everyone needs to learn is that do not be greedy or something like this could happen to you.

Jordan Thomas (12)
Cyfarthfa High School (Lower), Merthyr Tydfil

The Basilisk

Adam Richards walked quietly through the small wood, which was not too far away from his house. He was determined not to step onto the slippery ice, or wander off the path, which was leading him out of the park, as the fog seemed to be getting thicker. Suddenly, he stopped in his tracks as he heard an owl hooting not too far away. Birds flew out of their nests in the trees, and began to flap their wings, as they soared above his head in a huge crowd. Adam glanced at the sky, the clouds had disappeared, and it was the colour of navy blue. He knew that soon, it would be dark, and he knew that his parents would start to get worried if he didn't turn up at his usual time from football practise.

Soon, the sky had turned almost black, and tiny, silver dots began to appear, like glitter sprinkled on black velvet, and it didn't take Adam long to realise that he was lost.

He wandered for what seemed to him like an eternity. He realised that he wouldn't be able to get out of the woods until morning came. Adam clutched his pocket knife, which he always carried everywhere with him, as he started to see some sort of an opening somewhere. Soon, he realised, that it was a cave. He was happy that he'd finally found some luck, that night. He decided that he would sleep there and then figure out what to do when the morning arrived.

As Adam checked his watch, he found that it was almost half-past eleven, and he knew that it would take a lot more to get him to go to sleep that night. His eyes were wide open and his hands were clutched together, while shivering in the bitter cold. Suddenly, he heard a rumbling noise that seemed to be coming further into the cave. Adam stood up.

'Hello?' he called. There was no reply.

He began to climb over the large rocks until he seemed to be standing in a small, circular part of the cave. It was dimly lit by burning candles that were in each corner, and a fire was crackling in the middle. A hooded figure stood next to it. As soon as he saw Adam, he slowly got to his feet.

'Who dares to trespass here?' he asked in a very cold and unwelcoming voice. He pulled down his hood. The man's ugly face was covered with scars, his skin was almost green, and his cold, grey eyes glared at Adam's. He finally plucked up his courage to speak.

'Uh, I'm Adam, Sir. I'm sorry, I just-uh-got lost. So, I guess I'll just be leaving, then,' he said.

The man cackled nastily. 'Oh no you don't, dear boy. This is not a place you can just simply walk in and out of. There is certainly a punishment in store for you,' he said. He turned towards the roaring fire and muttered a few words, and Adam gasped as he saw a snake's head come out of the fire, followed by its long and slithering body. 'Let's see what the basilisk makes of you, shall we?' said the man as he pointed a long, pale finger towards him.

Adam began to run as the basilisk snapped its long, yellow fangs at him. He ran out of the room and tried to climb over the rocks as he could hear the snake's body on the floor. But he slipped, and fell on his back. Adam knew the basilisk was right behind him. As soon as it came towards him, with its mouth wide open, he grabbed a heavy rock and thrashed it at the snake. He knew that he now had time to run. He managed to get over the rocks and sprint as fast as he could. It was clear that he hadn't injured the basilisk, as he could hear it coming right behind him.

Adam was almost out, now. But suddenly, he tripped, and his body landed on the floor with a thud. He felt something slide out of his pocket. It was his pocket knife. Once again, the basilisk came sliding towards him. Adam grabbed the knife and thrust it into the snake's body.

The ground shook as the enormous creature hit the floor. Blood spilled out all across the floor. Adam's T-shirt was drenched in it. He could hear the man screaming at the sight of the basilisk's dead body, as he walked out of the cave.

When he was sure that he was far enough away from the cave, Adam sat down by a tree trunk. It was still a cold night. The sky was still black with silver dots, and the wind gently blew the leaves on the trees.

Suddenly, he heard a shouting sound. For the first time throughout that night, Adam smiled as he ran towards the sound of his father's voice, calling him.

Sara Jones (12)
Cyfarthfa High School (Lower), Merthyr Tydfil

Me, Myself And Ray

Great, my sister had won with her tantrum and we were off to the safari park again. I myself, would have preferred to go somewhere a little more exciting than off for the day looking at some dumb animals.

After what seemed like ages we finally reached the park, and despite my prayers it was still open. Dad made sure all the windows were shut and we started our 'safari' through the park.

'Oh look at the giraffes,' my mum exclaimed, as if they were the best things on the planet.

I sat in the back listening as Mum and Kelly cried, 'wow' and 'ahh,' at every sighting. I have to admit, I did get more interested as we approached the lion and tiger enclosures, I've always had a fear of white tigers so I needed to have my wits about me.

'Hold tight Rach,' my mother shouted as the car entered the first gate. I closed my eyes and slouched down on the seat, just peeking out now and again. Finally we were at the other end of the big cat enclosure, so I sat up straight as we approached the exit gates.

All of a sudden, everything stopped, my family were still and the car engine was silent. I looked around and everything was dead still and not a sound could be heard. I thought I must be dreaming, but I knew I was wide awake. Suddenly, I heard a sound. I looked around and saw a huge white tiger standing at the side of our car.

'Hello there Rachel,' the tiger said in a soft whisper.

I rubbed my eyes and looked again.

'Yes, I am talking,' he said, 'please don't be afraid.'

I thought that I must have definitely been sleeping then because I *knew* that tigers cannot speak. I stayed perfectly still and waited for my father to drive on through the gates and out of the compound. But the car, my father or my mother and sister didn't move and neither did anyone else.

'The name's Ray,' the tiger said.

I just stared out of the windscreen hoping to wake up any second. Suddenly the tiger was sat next to me on the back seat of our car.

'Don't be afraid Rachel,' he said.

'How do you know my name?' I asked him in a petrified voice.

He explained that every child born without a human twin has an animal twin instead, and he was my twin. I asked why he had not spoken to me on one of my previous visits to the park and he said that he had to wait for fourteen of our years before I would be able to understand. I asked why everything was still and he told me that 1 in every 4,000 animals have the ability to hypnotise people, and he had put everyone else in the park in a trance In order to speak to me.

'Fancy some real fun?' Ray asked. 'Everyone's asleep and we're in charge,' he said. Ray introduced me to his family and friends and we made our way to the fairground.

It was hilarious watching the giraffes on the water chute and the camels getting off the ghost train with their legs like jelly. The hippos threw a major tantrum because they wanted to ride the roller coaster but were told they were too heavy for the cars and track.

The monkeys were having a great time operating the rides, they loved teasing the other animals by starting and stopping the rides and changing the speed and direction every couple of seconds.

It was amazing to see the animals having such great fun. I'll never call them dumb again. It was an experience to watch them as they gathered around the ice cream stall to slurp and slop their lollies.

After what seemed like hours of fun and excitement, we returned to my car.

'Well I must be off now,' said Ray, 'and could you please tell Ian, the operator on the black fly ride that I've found you.'

I looked at him confused.

'He knows that when one of us finds a twin we love to use the rides, we don't do it very often but Ian will need to know where to find the things that the monkeys always hide,' Ray explained. 'What's that then?' Ray asked, eyeing up the sausage roll that my sister Kelly had in her hand. I told him it was her favourite snack just before he took it from her hand.

'What about my family?' I asked.

'You've got me now,' Ray said as he walked away, he turned and raised his huge paw as if to wave it. 'Bye Rachel,' he said and he trotted off.

Suddenly, everything was back to normal, my mother was pointing at the baby lions and going on about how cute they were. I looked around to check if I'd imagined it all and I saw Ray winking his eye at me. It was *real* and I hadn't dreamt it. Just then as I turned and smiled my sister yelled, '*Mum,* Rachel's stolen my sausage roll!'

Rachel Murphy (12)
Cyfarthfa High School (Lower), Merthyr Tydfil

The Giant Tooth Bite!

One day, not far from Merthyr Tydfil, something happened that I don't think anyone will forget. It was thousands and thousands of years ago.

A huge dragon with long, sharp teeth and fiery red wings came into Merthyr Tydfil and caused chaos for everyone in the town.

The dragon had travelled a very long way and was very hungry. First of all he went to all the farms and ate all the animals: the sheep, cows, hens, chickens and any other animals that the fierce dragon could find.

The dragon then moved onto all the farmers, the gardeners and all their families. After he had finished eating them he was still very hungry. He decided to go on another few miles and see if he could find a thing to eat there.

He found a lot of children and adults having a party on top of a mountain. He walked to the top where they all were and they ran as fast as they could away from him, but the dragon, being as big and as fierce as he was, chased them and ate everyone in sight.

The dragon was not as full as he wanted to be. He glanced around the town from the top of the mountain. He could see a black shadow behind a big, long stone wall.

Before he even thought what he was doing he took a big bite of the wall and fell to the floor making the town vibrate.

The little black shadow behind the wall was a young boy. He went up to the dragon, taking each step very slowly, and checked whether or not he was alive. He wasn't. The small boy looked around for a sharp stone. He cut the dragon's stomach open and everyone ran free. The young boy was a hero.

The giant tooth bite is still there today. When you are riding up the A470 just look up on the mountain and you will see the big giant tooth bite.

Sophie Jennings (11)
Cyfarthfa High School (Lower), Merthyr Tydfil

A Day In The Life Of An Ant

Today is another adventure. I wake up in my warm, comfy bed and the first thing I see is my beautiful wife, shouting at me to get up and find the family some breakfast. So I rub my tired eyes and get up.

I head off for my journey, the only thing I can think of is getting back home to my family, safe and sound. Whilst on my journey I stop and talk to my old friend Jim who I haven't seen in ages. We tell each other about our families. Jim's sister, Lucy, has just had a baby girl.

I look at the time and tell Jim that I have to go. Whilst I'm looking for food, the floor starts vibrating. I think to myself, *please don't be humans.* I look up slowly and see this huge, gigantic foot coming towards me. I run and run as fast as I can but the feet keep getting closer and closer. My heart is beating faster and faster. Then all of a sudden I see a small hole in the floor, so I dive in to it.

My heart still pounding I peek up to see if the human has gone . . . and he has. I climb out of the hole and see this huge piece of biscuit, enough to feed the whole of my family. I pick it up and head back home.

When I arrive home, I place the biscuit on the table and my family thank me. We all sit down to dinner and then watch 'It's A Bug's Life', the film. After the film we all go to bed and I tell my wife all about today. Hopefully tomorrow will be just as good as today.

Sâra Jones (13)
Cyfarthfa High School (Lower), Merthyr Tydfil

A Day In The Life Of The Queen's Favourite Corgi

Mmm, breakfast. Chunks of delicious dog meat - my favourite! I can't wait until my mistress wakes up, as she always fusses over me in the morning. I heard yesterday that the English rugby team are coming for a photo shoot later and I've just got to see them. Maybe they'll give me one of their rugby balls to keep because I'm so lovely?

Oh, hooray! My mistress is awake and what's that . . . she's putting on her coat and holding the lead. But she never takes me on my walks, one of the servants does. Maybe she's got time today to take me out. I hope she has, she's so special, my Queen is.

Yes! Great! She is taking me on my walk. I think we'll go around the gardens. I haven't been there for ages so there might be some new smells.

We are going around the palace grounds, and what's that she's saying now . . . she's doing a speech today in front of the palace and I'm to go with her! Cool! I haven't done that many times. I love my mistress.

The rugby team is here now and they're just sitting down. Maybe I can sneak into one or two photos. Oh yeah, Jonny Wilkinson's just picked me up and I'm going to be in the photo on his lap. It's a good thing we corgis are small - he'd never have picked me up if I were a Great Dane! I can't wait to tell all my brothers and sisters. They'll be *sooo* jealous!

Time for lunch and I managed to lick up a few crumbs from the floor. I think the Queen had a beef dinner . . . well that's what it tasted like anyway.

I'm really getting excited now. The speech is starting in ten minutes. I might be asked for my autograph from the other dogs at the do.

She's started now. I don't know how she does it. She always speaks so clearly - I know I'd mess it up if I'd done it.

Oh, whoopee! I'm getting loads of attention. Practically everyone is stroking me. I feel so popular!

Ah, snooze time - paradise! No need to run around any more. It's been a good day today, with all that's been happening. The English rugby team coming, the Queen's speech and especially the walk with the Queen. It is nice to be part of it all but sometimes it's too much, so that's why I'm snoozing, to get away from everyone for a while.

You know, corgis were bred in Wales to herd cattle and guard the village. Hmph - you wouldn't catch me herding cattle, but I suppose I do sort of guard the Queen, I mean I'd give my life for her.

And guess what? Corgis are known to be very intelligent, so that's probably why I'm so clever. We've been royal companions for years and we love being with people, especially children.

Da, da, da, daa, da, daaaa . . . What's that? It must be the changing of the guards. I watch them every day. Wow! Just look at them. Their uniform is so smart. I'd love to have one like that and definitely the big hat. It's amazing to think that they do this just for the Queen. It shows just how important she is! There are soldiers on horses now. They scare me quite a bit because they're so big. They could probably squash me easily.

Woof, woof, woof . . .

Oh no, not Rex again. That's Princess Anne's bull terrier and boy is he scary. I think I'll just go back into the other room and pretend to be asleep in my basket. I don't like him very much. He terrifies me even though he's not allowed to hurt me. Phew, he's gone. Now I can relax again. Perhaps the cook has got some tasty bits for me to nibble on before I go out for my last walk of the day. I love night-time in London because the lights are beautiful and you can hear a little buzz of the traffic going by and the ducks in St James' Park settling for the night.

It's the Queen's birthday next week. I wonder what I can give her? A fresh bone, my best rubber ball, some of my posh dog biscuits . . . *Zzz zzz.*

Rachel Phillips (12)
Cyfarthfa High School (Lower), Merthyr Tydfil

A Day In The Life Of A Dog

I woke up in a fright from my terrible dream whilst sniffing a waft of a delicious cooked dinner passing my nose. My nose felt different. I gave it a twitch. It didn't feel normal. I licked my lips. My tongue seemed longer. It felt hairier around my mouth. I started to get worried when I spotted I had paws and a tail and ears that hit my sheets when they flapped. I was red and white, I was covered in hair.

As I walked into the living room, I found it hard to walk on four paws. I kept tripping over my own feet. I finally found it, on the lap of my brother, the delicious smell. I sat there begging for a taste. That's when it hit me, I couldn't speak. I sat there drooling, hinting for him to give me a share, but all I could get was a crumb that had fallen out of his mouth.

Bang, bang! came a noise from my mother banging a spoon on the side of my dog's bowl, that's how my dog would know when her food was ready. I ran into the kitchen as my mouth watered. I tried to use my paws to eat my food, but I couldn't, instead stuck my head in the bowl and tasted the most disgusting taste ever. I thought to myself, *how could you like such a thing?* It was like eating grass. It was chewy and as hard as a rock.

Zzzzzz! I fell asleep, one of dogs' main hobbies. I hoped that I would become human in the matter of an hour. I hoped that I would wake up as one.

I was awakened by the feel of something slipping over my head. Then I guessed, a collar, I was going for a long walk up the field. I sprang and ran in, out and over the grass, feeling the coldness of it hit my legs. I stopped ever so suddenly, and felt something cold and wet come from underneath me. I was embarrassed, I was going to the toilet outside. When I had done what I had to do, my father took me home.

I stepped into my box as the night became young and hoped that my day would be different tomorrow. I hoped I'd have two legs not four, different and smaller features on my face and that I was a human. *Zzzzzz!*

Chloe Reynolds (13)
Cyfarthfa High School (Lower), Merthyr Tydfil

Head First

I woke up to the sound of singing birds that nested in the oak trees opposite my garden. It was a summer morning in the holidays. It was the day I was wishing for. I was going to the museum with my parents. For as long as I could remember I had been interested in paintings and artists. Just going to the museum was a privilege, I hadn't been in ages.

'They've finally produced an art exhibition,' I yelled. I had written to the board of directors about four times asking them to put on an art exhibition.

After a 20 minute drive to Cardiff the museum was eventually in sight. I slammed the door of the car and raced up the stone steps.

As I ran, I did so under the battle engravement. It was famous for its ancient markings. James I held a boy's head in his hand. No one knew if it was true. We had agreed in the car that I was to go to the gallery on my own whilst my parents had tea and coffee in the Grand Café upstairs.

So, that's what happened, I slumbered into the Westside Gallery full of famous statues made of clay and invented by different kinds of artists. One of the structures looked like a cross-section between a tiger and a hawk hunting for its prey.

Suddenly, I realised that this part of the museum was empty and dead quiet. The wallpaper was black and most of the sculptures were white and ghostly. Then, a shuffling noise coming from a corner on the far side caught my attention. I walked over nervously. It looked as if a statue had been pushed over by something.

I bent down and picked it up by the neck, a liquid spilt onto my hand. I held it up to the light so the watery substance shone. It dripped to the floor. 'Blood,' I screamed.

Suddenly, I heard faint noises in the background. Clashes of swords and desperate cries of men. The cold air brushed against my cheeks, making shivers run down my back.

I was standing in the middle of a battle scene, holding a boy's head. I was standing in shining but heavy armour. I looked up to the head. It was mine!

Luke Hier (12)
Cyfarthfa High School (Lower), Merthyr Tydfil

Young Writers – That's Write! Write Up Your Street Vol I

33

A Black Day At Monmouthshire

It lay there, its black tail curled on the ground. Blood dripped from its mouth. Bite after bite it sank its teeth deep into the woollen flesh of its kill. Tired from its labours the panther sat still, sniffing the air as if using its sixth sense. It knew I was there. I tried to slow my breathing ready for the money shot. My telescopic lens glinted in the early Monmouthshire dawn and the beast was off.

Sprinting across moorland and heath I followed my quarry, passed stone boundary walls and oak trees. The speed of the animal was amazing. Such agility and awareness gave nature's greatest predator an advantage over me, his pursuer.

To kill such a magnificent specimen seemed harsh, the bounty on the head of the lamb killer a bloody reward to a trained marksman.

We raced in tandem until finally the beast ran out of energy. My jeep slowed to a halt and I raised my rifle once more. I took aim and paused. Out of the corner of my eye I discovered why she'd stopped at this thicket. A second black shape appeared in my sights. It was a vulnerable cub. The thought of one thousand pounds crossed my mind but I could not do it. Something inside me told me as a mother myself, that I should not pull the trigger. A shot rang out across the silent valley. The previously vibrant black shapes crumpled to the floor. The next view I saw through my sights was that of a triumphant farmer whose sheep dog finished the job. I lowered my rifle in shame at the spectacle. It was a black day at Monmouthshire.

Jack Evans (12)
Cyfarthfa High School (Lower), Merthyr Tydfil

Time Of The Dead

(Based on 'Time For The Dead')

Every year at a special time, I would go and get my family into my lounge and tell them to remember our relatives, like my dad. We all sat on the big five seat sofa with the TV on at full volume. We were thinking about only one person, the most special person, my dad, who sadly only died yesterday, remembering. Remembering. Remembering . . .

My dad was dying, he had been dying for months now, he was meant to live for another couple of months, well, that was what the doctors and nurses said anyway. He had cancer, which was what had made him die, because he had a habit of smoking. He would have about fifty cigarettes a day, and, he is dead now even though he only lived until he was thirty-nine. My family always told him to stop, but he never did. Our family wanted him back so much, not just for the company but to tell him 'I told you so!' because all my family ever did was say that he would die if he kept on smoking fifty cigarettes a day and that it would make him die sooner, and at a really young age. I sometimes wish that he just never started smoking in the first place, because it has just ruined his life and more importantly my family's lives as well.

We will always know how stupid and unhealthy it is to smoke. I know now that it is dumb to smoke and so do all of my relatives. I know that I will never smoke; I'm just hoping that none of my friends and family will either.

Gareth Jell (11)
Dame Alice Owen's School, Potters Bar

Young Writers – That's Write! Write Up Your Street Vol I

35

New Version Of Ragharok

One day in march 2005 Tony Blair and Gordon 'Gordie' Brown were messing around on the computers which was what they were usually doing on Mondays before going to a press conference, then reporting to George Bush for more orders.

Tony decided to consult his new computer for info on Senator Kerry though he knew he would get the usual stuff. Suddenly a thought struck him, what if he looked in the police database it might have something on him. *Just a quick upload, download and a short virus scan and I'm in to the police database,* thought Tony. Then he looked at the screen and noticed that this wasn't the usual screen he remembered from when he got Bush out of trouble once. This was MI6, he had hacked into MI6 he was a genius, an absolute genius everyone would bow down before him!

Gordie coughed twice signalling his return, he had gone out for a cup of tea. *'Wow!'* cried out Gordie who just had a look at the computer monitor. '£3 for 3 games now that's a deal you don't wanna miss out on! Oh and MI6 database, someone up there is making this our lucky day.'

Tony had to read the sentence over 3 times to get it through his head, he looked at the little film about England's future and began to weep. On the screen he had a look at a barren wasteland with the occasional sign saying *Welcome to New York* or *London, England's Hub* all mixed on the world to be. But in the depths of the horror he saw a family huddled tight together searching for food. They stumbled upon a lush green woods and Tony realised that they are much older now and realised there is hope for mankind. It is in *rebirth*.

Matthew Nairne (11)
Dame Alice Owen's School, Potters Bar

The Tower Of Babel - A Hebrew Myth

Early in the morning of the world, the usual traffic and the rush to get to work; there were these builders who were sent by the government to build a new city. A city of bricks and cement. When the city was built, the builders were pleased and proud of what they had done. It was not like something they had built before, no of course not, this city was different . . . and do you know why? They had built a tall building at the heart of the city; it reached high into the heavens above.

This did not make God very happy, he was angry that people could now see so far upwards. In his fury, God stamped hard onto the earth and the tower of Babel collapsed as if a bulldozer had come to demolish it. All the hard work went down with the tower. The builders tumbled, the people fell. Their cries and screams were different, nobody could make out what each other was saying, and different words were coming out of individual mouths. One builder could not make out what his colleague was saying, one woman kept trying to say something to her husband, but he was puzzled and did not listen.

The city and the tower were never rebuilt, for we were split with different languages and countries and cannot understand each other. and that was that.

Zoë Johnson (11)
Dame Alice Owen's School, Potters Bar

Greedy Gonzalez

(Based on the legend 'Koobar the Koala')

In the year 3298 it was the first commercial flight of the Boeing 19,000,000 mark two (the Boeing 19,000,000 mark one had ended in disaster).

They were 30,000 feet up cruising over North Africa, which was in the middle of a drought. Multi-billionaire Sanchez Gonzalez was looking out of the window from his first class seat sipping the most expensive champagne.

In the pilot's cabin the dials suddenly started going mental and the pilot heard the noise that all pilots fear, it was the stutter of the engine! The plane started to fall and crashed into a tree! Only ten passengers and the pilot survived!

A few days later everyone went off to look for food, having hidden the little food that remained from greedy Sanchez! They went off in different directions and as usual Sanchez returned early trying to find the hidden food. Luckily for the others he didn't find it.

The next day however when they went off for water they forgot to hide the food. When Sanchez returned he found the food and greedily ate it all. He realised what he had done so tried to find more food to cover up his deceit.

A few minutes later the others came back and saw him halfway up a tree picking poisonous berries. They shouted madly at him. This made Sanchez lose his balance and fall out of the tree to his death.

They stood around the still body lying in a strangely crooked position. All of a sudden his body started shrinking and before anyone knew what was happening he had turned into a cross between a weasel and a small fat rat.

He looked up at them, 'Always leave food out for the animals otherwise I will make a huge plague sweep through your lands.'

From that day on crumbs were always swept off the table and left for the animals.

Sandy Kiddle (12)
Dame Alice Owen's School, Potters Bar

A Modern Version Of Daedalus And Icarus

One day Tony Blair and George Bush wanted to go to Iraq and find the weapons of moss destruction so they could get rid of all the evil moss in the world.

George said, 'We can't take the plane or the whole world will know what we're doing.'

Then Tony, being as clever as he is, had the idea of phoning Gordon Brown to tell him to think for them. Gordon suggested raising taxes.

'No!' shouted Tony and George.

Then Gordon thought of being able to fly without a plane. So he said, 'Why don't you make wings? Ha!'

He was joking but the other two thought it was a good idea.

'Yeah, well done, Gordon!' they said. Gordon was satisfied with himself so he thought he might add in the idea that they could also raise taxes. 'No!' they said again.

So the next day Tony and George went out all over the country trying to find feathers for two pairs of wings. Eventually they gathered enough feathers and headed back to number 10. They bought some wax and using that, they placed the feathers in position. But it wasn't easy. For them it was like trying to go outside without being harassed by a fellow citizen.

After all the pain the wings were finally ready, so they went to the highest cliff they could find and without even thinking they jumped off the edge. That wasn't very clever because George nearly landed in the sea but he was able to recover (oh well, better luck next time). They landed in Iraqi territory, but as soon as their feet touched the ground they were ambushed by the moss destruction company. The Iraqis said they would kill them if we didn't pay a ransom of £500,000. Of course we said no. Even if they had asked for 20p we still would have said no and let them suffer.

Zeynep Livatyali-Esen (12)
Dame Alice Owen's School, Potters Bar

Young Writers – That's Write! Write Up Your Street Vol I

39

The Cabalote Monster - The Loch Ness Monster

In the southern east of Taiwan, there is a small village called Cabalote. In the centre of Cabalote, there lies the deepest well in all of Taiwan - the Cabalote Well.

Legend has it that in the depths of the murky gunge at the bottom of the well, people believe that there lives a monster. They call it . . . The Cabalote Monster!

Nearby, there is a large high street packed with tourists from all over the world, here to catch a glimpse of the Cabalote Monster. There are gift shops and souvenir shops that sell toys of the monster and what the people of Cabalote think it looks like. People claimed to have seen it, there are faded photos of a dark figure lurking at the bottom, but the well is 70,000km deep and it's impossible to see the bottom.

One day a brave young girl wearing a blue hat dived in to find the monster. People called after her but there was no reply, then they saw a hint of blue and her hat floated to the top. Some think she was eaten, or drowned. Some think she is still on her way to find the monster.

Tanya John (12)
Dame Alice Owen's School, Potters Bar

Pygmalion

Pygmalion was the king of England and he was one of the best kings to ever rule England.

One day the king was terribly shocked when a beautiful English woman had brought public scandal to the City of London. Pygmalion was so shocked he retired into Buckingham Palace and decided to live there alone, free from the company of women.

The king was an artist, he loved carving sculptures. One day when he was working he suddenly decided to make for himself a sculpture of the perfect woman.

Pygmalion then took a piece of ivory and began to carve. When he was finished the statue was more beautiful than any woman in the world.

Pygmalion loved his ivory sculpture so much that he would admire it every day. He soon fell in love with his sculpture so much that he would kiss it. Sometimes he would kiss the sculpture and imagine that it was alive.

He bought lots of presents and jewellery for the ivory sculpture because he loved it so much. He would sometimes lay it down on a sofa and dress it in different gowns.

Pygmalion loved the statue so much that he kept wishing that it would come to life.

One day Pygmalion was going to see the theatre production of *Mamma Mia!* when he accidentally bumped into a beautiful young lady who looked exactly like his ivory sculpture.

Pygmalion was so amazed that he started talking to the young lady, they got along very well and they became great friends, then lovers.

They soon got married and had a child. The child was named Paphos, which is now a city in Cyprus.

Dionne Findley (12)
Dame Alice Owen's School, Potters Bar

Young Writers – That's Write! Write Up Your Street Vol I

41

Theseus And The Shotgun

A long time ago on the Island of Crete lived King Minos and his children. One of his children was normal and her name was Ariadne but one was a deranged loony who wore a bull mask over his head and he was called Minotaur. Every nine years Minotaur needed to eat seven men and women. So Kingy sent for the people.

One of the people who was going to come was a body builder named Theseus. Theseus' father was king of Athens and said, 'Thee, Thee I will phone you after a day to see if you're OK. If you don't answer I'll come over and check on you.'

'OK,' said Theseus, staring at a girl taking off her shirt.

So Theseus went into the labyrinth looking for the deranged loony. He found it. It charged at Theseus. Theseus pulled out his shotgun and blasted the Minotaur to Kingdom Come (which was about a mile away). Theseus then got carried away with his new toy. The shotgun. He began to blast his way out of the labyrinth.

Outside the maze the phone rang. It was Theseus' dad, but Theseus was too carried away with the gun and blasted the phone. Then Theseus' dad came, but Theseus killed him. Then Theseus planted an atomic bomb on the island and just as it was about to explode he grabbed Ariadne and used a jet-pack to get off the island.

Daniel Garber (12)
Dame Alice Owen's School, Potters Bar

My Version Of Icarus And Daedalus - John And John Junior

There once lived a boy called John. John was extremely clever. He grew up to be an amazing architect. He loved his son JJ (short for John Junior) very much.

One day an evil, professor kidnapped them because he wanted to be as clever as him. He forced John to build a brain switcher machine. 'You are scum, build me a machine or I will feed you and JJ to my piranhas,' said the professor.

'Okay, just don't hurt my son,' John said. He was scared and he felt trapped, he wanted to escape.

One day when the professor was sleeping, he stole some parts of the machine and he built two jet-packs, so that they could escape out of the window. When the brain switcher machine was ready, John waited until midnight then he got the jet-packs and strapped them to his and his son's back.

'Don't do loop-the-loops because the engine will break,' John told his son. They soared into the night.

'Come back here, I'm not finished with you yet.' The professor's empty threats filled the air; John knew that he and his son were safe. JJ was so excited that he forgot his dad's warnings and twisted and looped.

'Noooo!' John cried out, but it was too late. JJ fell down into the professor's piranha pool, and was eaten alive. John wept bitterly, *why hadn't he listened to me?* he thought. He lived the rest of his life happily, but he always had a reminder at the back of his mind, he never forgot John Junior.

Hannah Chapman (12)
Dame Alice Owen's School, Potters Bar

Icarus And Daedalus

There were once two men, a father and a son, who were on the run from the police of New York City. The father's name was Daedalus and the son's was Icarus. They had just escaped from jail along with five others although the rest had been arrested by the police. Daedalus and Icarus were running across rooftops (jumping from one to another) with the police close behind, either on foot, in the air, in helicopter, or in police cars.

From above a voice screeched out, 'Stand down! Stand down!

Kapaz! A bullet streamed through the air and hit the rooftop.

'That was a warning shot, stand down or suffer the consequences!'

'Never!' Daedalus called. 'I'd rather die!'

Pang! Ping! Pang! The bullets showered down but Icarus and his father avoided them. Suddenly Icarus stood on the edge of the rooftop and called down to the police below. 'Take your best shot!' he called out smirking.

Pang! Pang!

'Can't hit me can you?' Icarus called laughing. He ran across the side of the rooftops ignoring his father's warnings.

'Keep trying!' Icarus taunted.

'Get down you stupid boy!' Daedalus shouted, reaching for his son, but as he did so a loud bang came from the helicopter above. The bullet streamed through the air and hit Icarus in the stomach. Blood shot out of Icarus' back and showered over Daedalus. Icarus stopped dead. His life flew past him in milliseconds. For Daedalus everything seemed to be going in slow motion. Icarus fell off the roof and onto the bonnet of a police car. A tearful Daedalus slipped away into the night and was never seen in New York again.

Chris Chick (11)
Dame Alice Owen's School, Potters Bar

The Story Of Why Not To Trust A Giant Robot

There was a huge war between Iraq and America. Saddam Hussain had stolen Mrs George Bush and America fought ten whole years to get her back. Many became bored and couldn't care less about Mrs George Bush and wanted her to die and others just liked war. After nine and a half years had gone by John Prescott, God of War, gave Tony Blair an idea to end the war (even though he secretly wanted him to die). Prescott's idea was to build a giant robot.

This Blair did and he and his fellow buddies in Parliament hid inside it and waited . . . and waited . . . and waited. Soon the Iraqis came across it on their daily scavenging of the town. They debated about it, and finally took the giant robot into the village. They placed it outside Saddam's house (which is a pretty stupid thing to do when you've got 5 parliamentarians inside it). Tony Blair waited till night then crept out and slaughtered all of Saddam's evil associates. He took Mrs George Bush, assassinated her husband and married her.

On their way back they came across a long, green, slimy, horrifying creature. No, it wasn't Michael Howard, it was the Loch Ness Monster. Now of course the odds of just 'coming across' a monster that man has searched for for hundreds of years is pretty preposterous, but there you go. The Loch Ness Monster lurched about trying to get at Tony and Cherie, but unfortunately, he didn't manage to kill Tony Blair. Alas, Tony and his handy gestures bored the Loch Ness Monster out of its skin.

Mark Whelan (11)
Dame Alice Owen's School, Potters Bar

The Ungrateful Mouse

There was once a family called The Robinson Family. There was one child Timothy Robinson and the parents Sophie and David Robinson.

One stormy, dark, cold night Tim couldn't sleep, so he began walking step by step down towards the kitchen. As he got closer to the kitchen he saw a small grey blur on the floor. He moved closer towards it and found that it was a baby mouse. As he knew how much his mother hated mice he was going to put the mouse outside, but the mouse whispered, 'Please don't put me outside in the cold I need to eat some food otherwise I will die! Please feed me then I will never bother you again!'

Tim said to the mouse, 'OK, I will feed you but you must then leave and never come back again as my mother hates mice!' He picked up the mouse and put it in his pyjama pocket. He walked over to the fridge and got out some cheese and nuts. He gave them to the mouse and they both said goodbye to each other. Tim went back to bed and the mouse left the house. Little did Tim know that the mouse had crept back in and made a house inside the wall. As the months went by the mouse would chew on the cables and eat all the food. The house was destroyed. The father, David, put mouse traps all round the house to try and capture the mouse.

One night Tim heard very faint squeaks coming from downstairs. He got out of bed and began walking down to the kitchen. He saw a mouse trapped in a cage.

'Please help me!' said the mouse. 'I didn't mean to destroy your house, please let me out and I will leave straight away.'

Tim replied to the mouse, 'I'm not going to let you out, last time I did you ruined my house. You shouldn't have been ungrateful or greedy because now you have nothing.'

Alexandra Maslen (12)
Dame Alice Owen's School, Potters Bar

The Terminotaur

One day King Minos of Long Island summoned the architect, Richard Rogers, to design him a fortress with many walls.

The king built this maze because Don, the Mafia leader, had kidnapped his son and inserted machinery into him, turning him into the Terminotaur. When the king got his son back and discovered he had become an evil beast, he hid him in the labyrinth. Soon the Terminotaur demanded human flesh so Minos sent for 70 young New Yorkers to be eaten.

The mayor of New York, Aegeus, told the story to his son Theseus who got on the next black ship heading for Long Island with 70 youths, to kill the Terminotaur.

When he arrived, Minos' daughter, Ariadne, saw him and whispered, 'I'll help you kill the Terminotaur if you take me back to New York with you.' Theseus agreed and entered the Labyrinth. Ariadne gave him a heavy machine gun and a long length of luminous wire. Theseus strayed through the dark maze, while the luminous wire trailed behind so he wouldn't get lost.

Suddenly an explosion shattered the wall. Arnold Schwarzengger was standing with a smoking rocket launcher. 'I have come back from the future, to terminate the Terminotaur,' droned Arnold.

'I'm here to slay the omen,' replied Theseus.

They walked through the maze and came across the Terminotaur. Arnold charged at the beast but it sent him flying. Theseus grabbed the rocket launcher and blew off its legs.

'Run, I'll deal with this guy!' shouted Arnold.

Theseus followed the wire to the exit. The Terminotaur crawled after him but Arnold shoved some C4 in its mouth and said, 'You are terminated!'

Just as Theseus left the Labyrinth, it exploded.

Theseus and Ariadne returned to New York and became the rulers.

Jack Tebbutt (12)
Dame Alice Owen's School, Potters Bar

The Typhonator

The earth goddess, Gaia-Bot, had many children. One of these children was known as the Typhonator. From a very early age Gaia would tell him stories about how Zeus, the programmer of all the gods, used to fight with her other children. So naturally the Typhonator's hatred for Zeus grew and grew as did he.

When the Typhonator was all grown up he was the most monstrous god of them all. Every god was afraid of him. Thousands of snakes protruded from all parts of his body and every one of them hated Zeus as much as he. When the Typhonator was big and strong enough he went out to fight Zeus, and by now, he was the size of a small mountain. Up on Mount Olympus they fought and, at first, Zeus struck him down to earth with an EMP bolt. Crashing down onto a mountain in Syria, he immediately regrouped himself and came back at Zeus gripping his arms behind him. Then he struck the EMP bolt from his hands and tore the sinews from his limbs so that he immobilised and then he dragged Zeus off to his radioactive cave.

He gave the sinews to a creature who was half woman and half snake and told her to hide the sinews under a bearskin rug, but two gods flew down from Mount Olympus to rescue Zeus. They confronted the guards and did battle with them with amazing Matrix-style, wall-flipping and no-handed cartwheels. Then they faced the snake lady and while one of them distracted her, the other took the sinews from under the rug. The swiftest of the two flew inside the Plutonium-walled cave and returned the sinews to Zeus. Then they flew him back up to Mount Olympus.

Zeus, once again, attacked the Typhonator but, this time he threw a large piece of volcanic Syria over him. The Typhonator was crushed but, trapped desperately in the molten lava, his last words to Zeus were; 'I'll be back.'

Joel Stern (12)
Dame Alice Owen's School, Potters Bar

The Modern Version Of Theseus
And The Minotaur

He was an MI6 agent. Theseus was the name. There were seven women and seven men being held hostage by five terrorists, using the name Minotaur. Theseus went down to the old pub where the hostages were being held. He was told that if he rescued them he should fire a yellow flare and if not a red flare. A failed rescue would mean giving the terrorists the ransom they were demanding.

He looked through the window and saw four of the terrorists drinking and watching TV. While they weren't looking he went through the open gents' toilet window. Then, he made his way to the door where the hostages were tied up. He opened the door, cut their bonds and led them into the gents' toilets.

They all climbed through the window into a type of courtyard, which was quite small. There was a door. He tried to open it but it was locked. Fortunately, a woman came out and said she'd open the door if Agent Theseus would take her with him. They got into the helicopter and drove off leaving the woman behind while she went to get spare guns.

Whilst Theseus was in the air, he fired a red flare from the flare gun. MI6 thought he hadn't managed to rescue them, so they drove to the old pub and gave the 10 million pound ransom. The terrorists left in a helicopter while MI6 looked for the hostages. Agent Theseus came in with the hostages. He had fired the wrong flare.

Andreas Koulaumas (12)
Dame Alice Owen's School, Potters Bar

Young Writers – That's Write! Write Up Your Street Vol I

49

A Tragedy With No Theory

Two weeks wed, a couple from England were walking through Central Park at night; tomorrow they would fly back to their homeland. The honeymoon had flown by like the wind. Soon they would be thrown back into the stressful reality of life. Though what they didn't realise was that reality would come much sooner than planned . . .

Suddenly, a torrent of water came from the lake and stole the woman into its depths. The man was left alone, until another surge of water gave him a second drenching, but an enormous, monstrous creature came with it! A mighty jaw dived at the man, and it almost took him too, but he fought till he could fight no more! His efforts weren't without just reward though, for in the end the creature retreated, and turned away with a supreme swipe of its lethal tail, back into its murky lair.

This exciting new story put the press in a frenzy, but the widower was so forlorn that he locked himself away from the world and everyone in it. He flew back to England a month later, alone and depressed. After signing the legal documents, his flat in Ealing became his refuge. There was no body found in that lake, no trace of any carcass.

He only ever came out of that flat for the bare necessities, and God forbid any other soul than his cross through the threshold during the remainder of his lonely lifetime. Family were forgotten, along with friends, but in America, an investigation had begun.

Many were now reporting sightings of the beast, but after the first twenty-odd, the FBI got suspicious and closed the case. A mystery never to be solved, they said. Part of life is wonder: questioning a theory. So what do you think really happened?

Jenny Welch (12)
Dame Alice Owen's School, Potters Bar

An Unforgotten Day . . .

September 11th

Dear Diary,

Today is the day . . . the day we strike Iraq! It is a day that will be recalled through the ages . . . and I am part of it!

I am an American soldier and my fellow soldiers and I are going to give the Iraqis, what we soldiers call 'a good American warning'. We leave for Iraq in thirty minutes. I am sitting here worrying, like I have done for the past few weeks, wondering should I be doing this? I think how the Iraqis would be getting on with their lives . . . and then their world suddenly torn apart by a group of vicious, heartless, bloodthirsty people! I am usually convinced I am doing right by Commander Geary's speeches in which he always says; 'it's them or us'.

Commander Geary is a loyal American citizen and despises the Iraqis, he once addressed them as; 'a tribe of life-snatching addicts'.

Well I just hope . . .

Continued eight hours later

. . . *Boom! Crash! Thunder!* The whole camp shook like a leaf! I jumped up as quick as lightning and dashed outside to see what the horrific noise was . . . there before me was the most horrendous, disturbing sight I had ever seen . . . a cloud of smoke burst into the warm air . . . then suddenly a fighter plane smashed into the one remaining tower! I watched with an open mouth, the ghastly image before me! It was just then when I recalled Commander Geary's true words; 'it's them or us', and today it was us.

Louise Henderson (13)
Newtownhamilton High School, Newry

The Farm House

One day Billy the goat was waking up when something caught his eye, it was red and shiny.

Bertha the pig got up and saw it too and asked, 'What is that?'

'It looks like a new tractor,' Billy replied.

Redgie the rooster and Wilma the hen got up too. Wilma was a weird hen and had short-term memory.

'What is that?' said Wilma.

'It's a tractor,' yelled Bertha. 'I want to have a go on it.'

'Okay we'll all go on it,' said Billy.

So they went and got on the tractor and headed off down the lane, The farmer ran out and screamed and shouted and yelled at the animals.

Bertha yelled, 'How do you stop this thing?'

'I don't know, *look out!*' screamed Billy.

'Argh!' they all screamed.

Bang! They hit a tree, all of them ran back to the shed.

'That's the last time I'm ever going on any vehicle, I hate them. Oh look a jeep, let's go for a spin,' said Wilma.

'No way!' screamed Bertha.

Dean Maxwell (13)
Newtownhamilton High School, Newry

Treasure Underground

One day during the summer holidays I had arranged to meet my friends. As the day went on one of the boys thought it would be nice if we could meet up again before the holidays ended. He suggested we go to the cinema some evening. A date and time was decided and transport arranged.

We met up outside the cinema. We were going to see a film called 'Treasure Underground'. The film was about five boys called Jim, Bob, Jack, George and Phil. The boys were staying on a farm. There was a castle on a field belonging to the farm. They went to see a man who owned an antiques shop. The man was able to give them some old maps of the castle. By looking at these the boys found out there were dungeons under the castle. By studying the maps more, the boys found that a underground passage ran from a old storehouse in the middle of the farm to the dungeons of the castle.

The boys found a trapdoor leading underground. They decided to explore. The passage went steeply uphill and they walked for about 10 minutes before coming up against a door. Bob pushed the door and it fell over. Inside the door were chests and cupboards. The boys opened them and found they were full of gold and old swords.

The boys ran back down the tunnel to the farm and told the farmer and he called the police. When the police arrived and saw the treasure they said it would belong to the crown. The boys were still rewarded and enjoyed the rest of their holidays.

Simon Knight (13)
Newtownhamilton High School, Newry

The Winning Ticket

He sat in his armchair waiting patiently for the lottery results. The tea he had just made sat on the small table beside him, the steam was rising out of it and the blazing fire was warming his feet. He glanced at the letter he had received earlier that day from his daughter in Australia. She had requested him to visit her in the summer. How he longed to have a holiday to sunny Australia to get away from the bleak, wet weather over here.

Finally the programme was starting. Every Saturday night he watched this same TV show hoping maybe he could win some money. Except he had been doing this for so long he did not believe he could possibly win any money. The lottery numbers were being called out, '7, 25, 46, 13, 2, 51,' she said in her high-pitched voice. Then he looked down at the thin, crumpled paper and read the numbers. It read exactly what she had called out. He couldn't believe it! Then the bonus number was called out. '21,' she said. How lucky he was, he had matched all the numbers.

He cried out, 'I've won, I've won!' But there was no one there to hear him. How he longed not to be so lonely. Now he could visit his daughter.

Kathryn Jones (13)
Newtownhamilton High School, Newry

A Day In The Life Of . . .

You know when you get that feeling, that special feeling. Well that's what I had the other day. I still can't quite believe it! It happened overnight almost.

A couple of weeks ago I was at the beach just riding the waves and there was this guy who said I was really good for my age. I had never seen him before but there was this very dazzling boy who asked for the man's autograph and then mine. He said that one day I would be an international surfer, so could he have it now? I didn't know what to do but I gave it to him. (It's good to know you have one fan, who knows what could happen next.) I told my dad and my brother, all my brother did was laugh but Dad was really delighted for me.

Next morning, I was woken by the warm sunshine on my pillow and the smell of crispy bacon sandwiches. I got up with my special feeling inside. I had never had it before but that's what Mum used to call it. I put my green silky dressing gown on, Mum also said I looked like a mermaid. I smiled at myself, remembering all the little things she used to say. I got downstairs to a hero's welcome from Dad and Ed. I had no idea what it was all about until they handed me a letter. They said the guy at the beach had delivered it.

Rowan Toomey-Smith (13)
Oaklands RC Secondary School, Waterlooville

A Day In The Life Of Lizzie
(aka Queen Elizabeth I)

Oh how I do love a day frolicking in the meadows with my ladies in waiting! The exchange of love tokens each has been sent by a young courtier or a nobleman's son! Though my acquired passion is that of lingering for my lover to come and tempt me with his presence. He will not tell me his name for fear of my safety. Such a gentleman! The touch of his coarse stubble upon my soft and supple lips is thrilling but these heartfelt moments are limited.

These days are far behind us.

Many men came to my humble country abode, charging me with treason against, (dare I say it?) my own sister! I have never thought her heartless; I have always held my dearest Mary in high esteem for ruling this country so well. But now I can see she has truly judged and labelled me as my dearest mother also. She too was beheaded for no reason I see apparent. I fear this will be my end too.

I am now sitting on a flea-ridden bench with two of my dearest ladies plaiting my hair for the night's sleep. I am confident in saying it will not be filled with sweet dreams of my dearest lover, but of a nightmare screening of my own deathbed. Little did I know, as soon as I would awake, my sister's death would be publicised and the crown put upon my unknowing head.

Sophie Newnham (13)
Oaklands RC Secondary School, Waterlooville

A Day In The Life Of . . .

It felt like the air around me was so dense it was hard to walk! My father wore a navy blue suit and his thick black hair was scraped back with gel. He was marching along at such a pace, Saleema and I had to run to keep up with him. He kept a straight face showing no expression, but deep creases stretched across his forehead.

My mother was wearing a long deep red traditional Muslim dress and a black scarf was wrapped around her head.

As me and my sister scuttled along, my heart was thumping against my ribcage. It wanted to get out. It wanted to escape from this lonely teenage girl. My heart was reflecting my confused feelings.

I wanted to grow long white wings and flutter up to the sky, past the sky, away from this terrible, upsetting world.

As I looked at my sister I realised how lucky she was. She had not yet reached her teenage years and her hazel eyes showed a carefree, young, innocent girl.

'Hello Nadia.' A man walked into my path and gave me a half meaningful smile.

There, looking me in the eye, was my arranged husband. My wings were suddenly ripped off. There was no escaping. My life had come to an end.

Anna Wyatt (12)
Roundhay High School, Leeds

Young Writers – That's Write! Write Up Your Street Vol I

57

A Day In The Life Of . . .

I look all around me. I see trees becoming bare and there are few people out and about. It's a grey murky day. Miserable and depressing and believe me, I've seen enough of those this year.

I used to talk to my brothers and sisters, they used to live with me. They're dead now, I'm the only one of our family left. I never knew my parents, not properly. They left me a long time ago.

My life has been utterly boring, if I'm honest. I do nothing, I just sit here and watch. Day in, day out. Life doesn't change for me. My mood stays the same, even though I see happy people, sad people, loving people and people that hate.

I'm different to them. I know that all too well. You can't help what you're born as and it was my luck, or not, to be what I am.

Suddenly I feel like I'm being ripped apart. It doesn't hurt, it's an odd sensation. I suddenly see the branch that is my home, above me. As I slowly drift to the ground . . . I die.

Hannah Kelly (13)
Roundhay High School, Leeds

The Ghost Of Honeymore Hotel

Rickie and Jamie started unpacking their cases. Suddenly Rickie started giggling.

'What?' Jamie asked curiously. Rickie kept laughing and pointed towards a pair of flowery underpants that were lying in Jamie's suitcase. He quickly took them and stuffed them into a drawer. Rickie carried on laughing.

'Shut up, you pompous ignoramus!' shouted Jamie, going red with embarrassment.

'Hey, don't get your knickers in a twist, petal pants!' Rickie teased.

'Well, at least, I don't take a cuddly toy on holiday with me!' jeered Jamie, indicating to the stuffed animal on Rickie's bed.

'You leave Teddy out of this!' Rickie screamed.

'At least I'm not the one that smells like cat puke!' Jamie insulted.

This was too much for Rickie and he lunged at Jamie, to push him over. Jamie dodged and Rickie flew into the wall.

'Hey you broke the wall!' Jamie exclaimed, pointing at a big hole in the wall.

'That's impossible, the wall's made of brick! Anyway, I don't have a big head like you!' retorted Jamie.

'It's true, look, you have made a hole and it's hollow!' said Jamie.

'I wonder what's in there,' Jamie pondered. Where the wallpaper was torn away around the hole they could see the wall was made from wood and there was a keyhole below the hole. Curiously the pair pulled more of the wallpaper off to uncover an old, dusty cupboard.

'Let's look inside it!' said Jamie, hesitantly.

Rickie turned the rusty key in the lock. It began moving, clicking noisily. Both were silent, in anticipation of what was behind these mysteriously locked doors. Slowly Jamie reached towards the doorknob and they opened the door slowly, to reveal something grotesque and deadly frightening, that for a moment their blood ran cold before they could scream . . . 'A skeleton!'

Keith Organ (15)
The Barclay School, Stevenage

Mirrored As Equal

Theodore Brown was an ordinary man, a man living and working in 1955. He lived in a rundown area of Little Rock, Arkansas in America and had worked for everything he owned.

During this time black people were thought of as inferior and meaningless. So Theodore was lucky to have a job, it didn't pay very well and he got a lot of stick over it.

After three months of slaving away at a wage of seventy-three cents a week, for cleaning offices, he managed to save up enough to visit the junk shop to see if he could find any bargains for his one bedroom shack.

A day later, after work, he paid a visit to the junk shop that was situated four blocks away from his shack. Theodore had a good look around and was very careful not to miss anything. He was moving a few large boxes when he came across a mirror in the corner, it had a minor chip on the glass but nothing that couldn't be tended to by a bit of time and effort, so he purchased it for a tidy sum of four dollars. This was surely his best find yet. After walking the four blocks home he propped it next to his radio, a previous observant buy at seven dollars.

Theodore looked into the mirror with amazement as what he saw could have changed the world for blacks everywhere. What he saw was black men working side by side with white men. Black women shopping with white women, what he saw were the plans for the civil rights movement.

Justin Feller (14)
The Barclay School, Stevenage

Soldier At War

13th December 1944, war coming to an end. Well it should be after this invasion. I've been training now for six long and strenuous months, along with my comrades. The planes are ready. We should be landing at 6 o'clock local time in a small village called Cantane 12km west of Strasbourg. We will be landing right near a German stronghold.

The whistle blows, I pick up my luggage and my M6 Grand. I slowly climb up the stairs onto the B26 transport plane. On that plane will be the 64th Eagle Division.

Away we go, the planes accelerate. I push myself into the back of my seat, gritting my teeth. On the plane it is a very tense hour or two, not much talking. Private Allen and Private Stevens have already been sick.

The light shines red, I know what it means, time to get up. It shines like the tunnel to Hell. I take a deep breath and stand up. The sergeant tells us to check each other and then clip up, just as I hear from behind me, '9 OK,' the left wing is hit by AA fire. We have to jump or we will surely crash. The green light shines and there we go. As I jump out of the plane I slip and fall sideways. Oh no, there goes my gun!

I squeeze my fists in anger as I see it falling to the ground. I must be about 6,000 feet up so I will never find it.

I hit the ground, bending my knees. Two people land just near me. I think that they're both from the 62nd. The two look at me and make signals. I know what they want there is an AA gun just the other side of these brambles. I show them I have no gun but they have already gone. I have to follow. I crawl through the brambles and hear two shots. I jump up and there is a German pointing his gun straight at me and . . .

Richard Curtis (14)
The Barclay School, Stevenage

All Alone?

(In the style of 'Of Mice & Men' by John Steinbeck)

Everything calm, isolated and peaceful, all to be heard was the whisk, light clash of a tiny ripples from the fresh saltwater, lapping up against the smooth, worn down edge of the rock. The fine rays of the sun now faded into the deep golden grains of sand which the children once lunged the surface of their feet into, the prints have now become invisible. The light *coo* of the seagulls can be heard amongst the gush of the wind echoing in the distance. The burnished orange of the sun slowly lowers down until only the very tip can be seen, setting itself apart from the glowing colours of pink, red and faded yellows. Almost like a sinking coin fading away into the bottomless blues of the ocean.

As the sun lowered the wind seemed to become a bit stronger and as the night drew closer the crabs scuttled under the rocks, using the heat gathered from their shells in the day to insulate their bodies. Even the fish seemed to shiver as the water rippled and made tiny ringlets circling around bigger each time, as if trying to reach the edges of the rock pools. The beautiful silver coloured strips of the shells lay shimmering and glinting at the bottom of the pool, soaking up the last rays of the sun and reflecting out into what now no longer looked like a beautiful day but just a cool summer's night.

In the distance, up by the next set of rocks, a short, hunched up shadow emerged from the corner of a towering rock. A small, skimpy figure padded up the sands barefoot. He wore a shabby, dust-coated red peaked cap to one side and a pair of grubby denim-like dungarees with a grass-stained, once-white top underneath. As he marched up the beach he grabbed pebbles from the edge of the water and skimmed them powerfully into the very middle of the clear sea, using just a flick of his filthy palms to make them jump, not just once, but three times they'd hit the skin of the surface before plunging into the water. His frail figure seemed timid but the rough look he carried gave him that dangerous edge and made him look perhaps mysteriously handsome.

Jane Davis (15)
The Barclay School, Stevenage

The Next Chapter Of Nightjohn (Gary Paulsen)

I be learning for 2 hands and 4 fingers, Nightjohn say this be 14. It be a clear, starry night when we see the horror. In the moonlight we see blood on the walls. The pit be found, group be caught! I be shakin' but Nightjohn be calm.

'Go to quarters and prepare. We leave tomorrow. Tell no one.'

I be wanted leave so long, yet now I be sad. Sad. Describes my whole life.

Waller be looking at me strange. He be thinking something. My troubles! But he can't! He be dragging me to the hut if he knew. Strange. I must leave.

I tell Mammy. She start weepin' so I hug her.

'No, no. I be happy! Be free, be free!' she whispered in a sombre delight. 'But promise me one ting. When you be free, help us. You'll know how. Sarny, don't cry!'

'I'm not,' I say, feeling my tears.

It was dark, silent. I be running through the fields, Nightjohn behind. I look back; Nightjohn be gone. Hidden in the dark. Gone. I run by meself. Run and run. The smell of lard surrounds me. I now be free. Legs heavy I carry on. But I fall, collapse and sleep.

My eyes open to see Waller's ugly face. He got me, yet he be smile. No savage dogs. What's happening? The buggy nears the white house. Crap-face talks: 'They,' he points at the workers, 'they are proper black barbarians. You are different. You have as much white blood as black.'

What is he jabberin' on about?

He carries on: 'You can't learn from savages. You're staying with us!'

I look with disbelief at where I be livin'.

Chris Fawcett (12)
The Barclay School, Stevenage

The Choice

In the little village of Amroth-Upon-Glen, everyone agreed Justin Miller was a good Christian. Even the odd 'demon drink' was fine. One stormy night he entered the Jackal's Head. Outside stood five massive stallions. Inside it was full. A hooded figure waved him over to his table.

'Cheers. What a storm! S'like the . . .'

'End of the world?' the figure interjected. Justin talked for a long time with the man and his three companions. They worked in demolition. Charlie was thin and hungry; Aaron, loud and slightly annoying, Peter, angry and gruff and Bill, smooth and sly. Though strangers, they felt trustworthy.

'We're not religious men, Justin,' said Bill. 'If you'd seen what we have, you'd be an atheist. But the bad in the world will soon be done.'

'We'll have to go soon,' said Charlie. 'It's our one last drink before the big party.'

'Party?' asked Justin.

'Private,' smiled Aaron, 'but you're a decent man. The boss should let you come.'

They stood up and walked away.

Bill turned. 'Think about it,' he called and pulled up his hood.

Justin flinched as the skull shone through Bill's face. Alone in the pub, he pushed away his fifth brew.

He walked outside and saw . . . the *apocalypse!* Mountains of fire billowed in the roaring blackness. Then he saw the four unhooded, riding the air. *'This is the choice,'* they screeched, *'die a Christian now, or live in damnation forever!'* They rode and Justin noticed the fifth steed waiting . . . for *him.*

Steven Chamberlain (12)
The Barclay School, Stevenage

Satan's Star

('Creating a Monster' - in the style of Mary Shelley's 'Frankenstein')

As the trees encased me all I could see for miles around was seemingly black grass weaving between their trunks. Each of my steps was taken with caution, as I virtually reached my destination. Something startled me and my neck jerked clockwise. A screeching crack jolted my nerves as a vomit-like case of vines and skin caught my eye. It split and a 'starfish' dropped out.

As the wretch's body deposited into the ground its network of arteries and veins was definitive, the sick-like hide made me want to turn and dash away but I couldn't, it was too astounding. The creature lay, lifeless. It looked like a mutated brown-green starfish, hair sprouting between its tentacles. In the dead centre of the body lay a gaping mouth, not breathing, yet alive and horrendous. Its needle-like teeth lined the one circular gum. The mouth wasn't anything human-like but a hole, just a black, endless hole. Then it happened.

The creature sat up or slid up attentively. It glanced at its own body. Then its eyes (attached to the end of each limb) fixed on one solitary target, me. As it approached it seemed immortal, almost untouchable as if it could withstand a cavalry of rifles and cutlasses. It rasped like the wind rattling through dead leaves. Its movements quick and slug-like were enough to send a chill down any spine.

I had reached that moment, that point when I didn't know what emotion to feel - anger, amazement, fear - that was it. The only thing this monster was going to leave was a path of destruction. No, it couldn't be, nothing's unstoppable. But it must be. There was simply no time, it was there, right in front of me . . .

Steven Slayford (13)
The Barclay School, Stevenage

Creating A Monster

(In the style of Mary Shelley)

It was a dark, gloomy October evening when I beheld my much loved offspring's bewildered expression in his mother's warm, glowing living room. The date was October 31st, Hallowe'en to most, but to me, it was my son's birthday.

As his dear mother brought him into my presence, I simply gestured for him to sit down. I explained who I was and why he was here. I was growing weak and needed a successor, he was it. The reaction that followed was not expected.

Wings shot out of his back and his muscles, they bulged up from under grey skin, his clothes ripped. As my son flew up in the air, I gasped at his ragged wings and his perfectly formed clawed feet in admiration. It was more than I could ever have hoped for.

As the beast opened its dragon-like eyes it exclaimed, 'Why? Why did you keep this from me?' Yet its tremendous rage didn't stop it from being a spectacular creature. Every aspect of it, from its long, sharp claws to its ransacked wings which were glowing in sheer brilliance.

While the monster smashed his mother's furniture with ease, I began to wonder if breeding such a destructive being was such a good idea. It was as though I was actually feeling regret.

He was so consumed with his own wrath that he could, effectively, bring God down on his knees begging for mercy. Yet if I could harness the powers my son wielded, I could be the new God!

James Kirkpatrick (12)
The Barclay School, Stevenage

A Knock In The Night

Los Angeles was eerily quiet, night had done its duty and killed off the daylight and now had nothing to do but await its inevitable fate. Cops had closed the street and wandered around in the dark mist. The subway station had been closed due to the terrorist activity inside. *Four hostages,* the SWAT commander thought as his team stood by the entrance in their standard blue coveralls.

'Ten David to BCT TAC one, entry team stacked up and ready for entry. Go when ready.'

In response to the go-code, the officer led his team into the dark subway. Their gun-mounted flashlights carved through the darkness like a knife through butter. They headed for the platform via the stairwell.

'Bravo, enter and clear.'

Bravo moved. Nothing. 'Clear.'

The door at the bottom was locked. The SWAT leader could hear the terrorists. He froze. 'Stack up,' he ordered after a moment, 'breach, bang and clear. Go!'

An officer placed some C2 explosive on the door. The officers braced themselves. Two got ready their tactical grenades. The others clutched their guns. The SWAT leaders nodded as an officer detonated the C2.

'Door is breached.'

'Go!'

The door spun off its hinges in a loud sizzling sound. The SWAT team piled in, two at a time. the first two threw their projectiles. The others took aim. The flashbangs hit the floor in a loud, angry cry. Bright light shattered around the room, disorientating the terrorists. The SWAT team's MP5s fired in three shot bursts. Quiet. Fatal.

One tried to return fire. The hollow point hit him before he could depress the trigger. The terrorists fell around the confused and shaken hostages. It was over. The hostages were safe. For now . . .

Daniel Day (16)
The Barclay School, Stevenage

Miranda's Bar

The doors creaked as Vincenzo sauntered into Miranda's Bar. He paused in the doorway, before adjusting his fedora (covering one eye - how he always wore it) and glanced around the bar, taking in what he saw - the usual crowd of drunks and sleazebags were drowning their sorrows in the watering hole.

He walked over to the bar girl and asked for his usual Manhattan. He winked at the pretty black girl with his visible eye and flashed his most charming smile. She fluttered her eyelashes at him, returned the smile and . . . turned to serve another customer. Vincenzo shrugged. He wasn't bothered; he wasn't there for the girls anyway.

As he walked over to the prearranged meeting place, he saw two pinpricks of light glinting from the darkness. He took his seat anyway and removed his hat. He calmly tapped the button under the table twice - the signal for 'spy' for as long as he could remember. Even now Carlos and Marco would be getting ready for a fight if it came down to it. Vincenzo always felt safer if someone was watching his back.

After what felt like ages, his contact arrived. He looked nervous about meeting Vincenzo in such a situation, but then, he was relatively new to the 'business'.

'Do you have the information we asked for?' Vincenzo spoke in hushed tones.

'Well, yeah, but . . .'s gonna cost you . . .' the man *was* nervous.

Vincenzo decided to work this to his advantage. He leaned towards the man conspiratorially. 'Not as much as it'll cost your organisation if you don't hand it over,' Vincenzo rasped.

The man gave a terrified expression and handed over the envelope immediately. Vincenzo stood up, tossed the man two quarters and left.

As he made his way to his Mercedes, he felt eyes watching him. He stopped and listened hard. Whoever it was, they were directly behind him. Vincenzo drew his gun, spun and shot . . .

Molly Wilson (15)
The Barclay School, Stevenage

A Life In The Bronx

The evening is drawing nearer. As the sun silently retreats to the eternal blackness below, slowly, gradually, the shadows come out to play as the cover of darkness spreads like a thick mist over the sleeping city. Thus, a new world awakens.

They creep their way through every street and alley and conceal every crack and crevice, passing through every shattered window and creating a blanket over the glittering shards scattered across the pavement; stealing away their diamond-like quality. The darkness makes no exception to the Bronx.

A small, sharp yet distinguishable sound cuts through the silence, causing the mice to scuttle back through the rotting holes in the brickwork of the nearby rundown and abandoned housings, each one seeming to tower over the next. The noise was followed by another, and the faint silhouette of a figure appeared to materialise from the blackness.

The continuous rhythm of the hollow footsteps echo down the long stretch of the closed-in and noticeably narrow alley, located around the back of the main street, that was now silenced of its daylight cries.

Each path sent you deeper into its maze.

But one individual was oblivious to its twists and turns. He knew every shape; the way it seemed to merge into the next, every corner; where it would lead you and every danger; what fear could await you should you fall into the wrong hands.

The man lifted his head, just enough to see under the rim of his beige huntsman hat. His breath trailing behind him in the dense, winter air gave the only clue he was even there - completely submerged in the shadows, and spotted his target, standing under the dim light of the lamp post - just as he'd planned.

Samantha Foulds (15)
The Barclay School, Stevenage

Man-Eater

(In the style of Mary Shelley)

It was a dismal night in October. The rain hit the windowpanes ferociously, as the mist settled around the vast lab. I began to drink my warm cup of cocoa, but I still continued on with research.

The moon shone brightly through the window and I felt exhausted. I walked over to the creature on the table, the creature I had created. I was trying to create a son or daughter, someone who would love me for who I was. But I had made a monster. The beast could not love anyone and I definitely could not love *it*. I decided to call it a night and I would start again in the morning.

The next day the weather was the same. I walked through the door feeling excited but slightly apprehensive. As I turned to switch on the light with my back towards the table I said, 'Good morning my child,' but when I turned around the creature had gone. I quickly searched the lab with growing concern. It seemed as if he had just got up and walked off. *But how could he?*

Strangely everything went silent and a wind swept through the lab and I started to have the feeling that I was being watched. I slowly turned my head. I took a look out of the window. The mysterious woods next door made the atmosphere look even more daunting. Suddenly I heard a small cry. I turned around and there he was, my creation was alive. His large white eyes were hidden under the vast brown coat that covered him from head to toe. His strange, shadowy face lay silent, all was still. The creature began to shriek and was breathing heavily, he looked like he wanted something but I didn't know what. His large eyes stared at me. He raised his arms and slammed me against the wall. I gasped for breath, I started to fear that he was going to kill me. Suddenly his head fixed on the outside window. It was already 5am and the sun was beginning to rise. In a deep voice he said, 'We haven't finished here,' then he let go of me and quickly ran out into the misty forest next door.

That night I could not sleep a wink. I kept thinking about what he had said. Suddenly I heard a large crash on the door. I quickly put on my dressing gown and went downstairs. There was another large crash that made the wooden door splinter. He was trying to get in. A third crash sent the door to the ground.

In a menacing voice he said to me, 'I told you we had not finished. I heard what you said last night, that I would never love you but you created me, so I did, but now I think the opposite. I am going to make you suffer for what you did to me.'

This was it, we were going to fight to the death. With his sharp, bloodstained teeth and his razor-sharp claws, I knew I didn't stand a chance. The only thing I had created, the only thing that I ever loved was going to kill me . . .

Callum Baker (13)
The Barclay School, Stevenage

Ella

The Steps were going to some dinner dance thing held by Prince Dave to encourage him to meet some 'charming' young girls. I obviously wasn't invited (and didn't have anything long enough to wear anyhow) so decided to do the usual and make like a couch potato. Pop Idol was on and I had more chance being a diva than marrying that somewhat . . . unusual royal anyhow.

I had just settled in front of the TV (okay I'd been there an hour or so) when I got an odd feeling in the pit of my stomach - perhaps a whole tub of ice cream to drown my sorrows had been a touch over the top. The doorbell rang (very odd as I'd forgotten to change the battery). I ignored it. It rang again, I reluctantly got up and opened the door, expecting some pretty young thing wanting directions to the palace. I was surprised to see a rather more mature wannabe (arguably mutton dressed as the tooth fairy, a real no hope case).

'I know why you cry dear child,' she said with a smile which no self-respecting dentist could have seen for years.

Weird, I thought - they hadn't even started singing yet and I always enjoyed the bit where people got voted off. Aside from the indigestion I was feeling quite good. Then I remembered my dear father's words . . . 'Sorry,' I said, 'I really shouldn't talk to strangers.' I politely indicated to the front door, ushered her out and closed it behind her.

Pity, a few hundred years ago I might have been in with a chance!

Micha O'Neill (13)
The Barclay School, Stevenage

The Daywalker

(In the style of Mary Shelley)

It was an unusual day for summer, cold, dark and streets deserted. It was close coming to midnight on Friday 13th July, I knew something would happen. I was working on my creation, when I heard a sound. When I went to investigate I found him, the vampire, the missing link with his long fangs, black hair and long black cape combining him with others he would become the ultimate monster. He was saying that the castle was to be the new home of the vampire nation. He was the leader now he was perfect for my creation, then all that was left was to lure him to me.

I had to tempt him using my blood. He fell for it and followed, I had him now. He ran straight into my lab. He was trapped. I had a plan to capture him, a dart gun, the plan was a success. Then he awoke and found himself strapped to a chair. He had not fully recovered, so he did not struggle. Then by the time he recovered it was too late. I had already started the countdown . . . My creation it was transformed. He was reborn, but he did not seem pleased. He was furious and shouted that he would get his revenge. I had to run to get away, for the rest of my life I have to run and he is always chasing. My creation was a disaster. I had created a monster. A monster bred to kill.

Liam Boyce (13)
The Barclay School, Stevenage

Visit To Planet Earth

On this planet the people eat lots of different food. On my planet all we eat is chicken curry.

On Earth there are shops where people buy things with something called 'money'. On my planet we just take what we want. We don't need money.

Where I live we have 47 hours in a day but I have only been here 24 hours and one day has already gone. The humans go to sleep when it gets dark. There are bright dots called lights that use something called 'electricity'.

I landed in some green prickly things. I found out that they are called trees.

It is very hot and I like it because it is so cold on my planet. I want to stay on the planet but I will have to go home.

Kimberley Smith (15)
The Grove Special School, Berwick-upon-Tweed

Visit To Planet Earth

I landed in wet stuff which is blue, that humans call water. I floated to the beach, humans were having fun in the water and on the sand. I stayed out of sight because the humans will be frightened of me.

I went to the woods and the humans were watching the birds. I went to the swimming pool, the children were having fun in the water and the adults were speed swimming. I went back to my spaceship and I got my belt which makes me a human for 10 hours, then I went to the swimming pool and I went in the water and did speed swimming.

On my planet we don't have water. I went back to the woods then I watched the birds and I made a friend. I went back to my spaceship. I took some water with me to my planet. When I showed the other aliens they were pleased.

Shaun Graham (12)
The Grove Special School, Berwick-upon-Tweed

Young Writers – That's Write! Write Up Your Street Vol I

75

Something

I woke up and screamed, then my two friends Yazmyn and Sky woke. They whispered, 'Calm down Lola, it was only a nightmare.'

Suddenly we heard it. It was the clamp that we'd heard on TV, so we raced downstairs and went in the living room. No one was there, Sky turned off the TV and said, 'Who put the telly on?'

Smash! went dinner plates on the kitchen floor. We rushed there. There was a funny-looking thing, looking at us.

We walked back slowly to the stairs and ran up them. The thing slithered after us, we ran faster, the thing was trying to bash in, suddenly the floor fell down.

It got hold of Yazmyn and snapped her in half like a stick and went off. We phoned the police, but it was too late, the thing had killed everyone in the world, except us. Me and Sky.

Naomi Rawlings (11)
Threemilestone School, Truro

Record Results

On Tuesday 29th of June, terror struck as two of the Year Six teachers discovered that their pupils had the lowest SATs scores ever recorded.

Startled teachers spent the morning rechecking the results over and over again; making sure there weren't any precious marks that had been left out.

One of these teachers was Mrs Coleman who had just got back from buying rewards for the achievements the children had made (or so she thought). 'I thought it was unfortunate that the first paper had a bad mark on it, but when I looked through all of them, I was speechless to see they were all the same'.

Later that day, other fellow teachers found out the disgraceful results; and were horrified to think they were part of that school!

The next day, the school was horded by proud yet angry parents wondering how their children could possibly get these results.

It is still a mystery to everyone to whether the results were fake or the children were just hopeless!

Katie Bowen & Chloe Northover (11)
Threemilestone School, Truro

Young Writers – That's Write! Write Up Your Street Vol I

77

SATs Results Disappoint Children

The day came for results to be given out.

Yesterday, the 30th of June at 2.30pm the SATs results for Threemilestone Primary School were given out to the Year 6 children.

Some children were disappointed by the levels that they had. Some pleased the stress is over and done with.

The teachers were being begged by children for their levels. 'I'm glad we have got our results', says Naomi Rawlings being reported.

So the results are out, children happy, children sad. The stress of revision and SATs over.

Bryony Thomas (11)
Threemilestone School, Truro

Woodcutter Saves Riding Hood

The wolf, aged 65, died early this morning from being stabbed in the stomach with a knife and his house, 35 Trotters Lane, Newcastle is now being sorted.

The woodcutter broke through the front door of Grandma's house. He saw that the cupboard door was moving so he went over to see what it was. The cupboard was locked but there was still space for Grandma to be lifted out. The woodcutter lifted fat Grandma out of the cupboard. The wolf didn't know because he was fast asleep.

Previously, the wolf knocked on Grandma's door, pretending to be Little Red Riding Hood. Quickly, he chucked Grandma into the cupboard and locked it. He then put on Grandma's night-cap, nightie and glasses. Red Riding Hood ran through the door. She thought that Grandma looked very poorly that day.

Earlier, Red Riding Hood was skipping through the woods to get to Granny's house when she saw a wolf lurking through the trees. Red Riding Hood stopped to talk to him, but she just remembered not to talk to strangers; but still, she carried on talking to him. He raced on to Grandma's house to trick Red Riding Hood into thinking that he was Grandma.

Before hand, Red Riding Hood was playing in the garden when her mum said that she had to take a basket of food to Grandma because she was very ill. Red Riding Hood was warned not to talk to any strangers on the way.

Sophie Hay (10)
Threemilestone School, Truro

The Monster Man

A thousand years ago there was a man, but he was not an ordinary man, he was 14/6 feet tall. People did experiments on him, but the last went terribly wrong and he became highly mutated. He had the strength of a raptor, his body went blood-red. Worst of all he was invisible and terribly silent. He sought revenge on the scientists. They put him in a box, and set him out to sea.

In the year 3201 a family of four were on the beach in North California. The youngest girl tripped on what looked like a giant box. There was an inscription on the lid. XIII. Her dad pushed off the lid, but nothing was there, or that's what they thought. Soon they were hanging in the air, they were dead.

People all over America were dying. The scientists discovered a weapon to destroy the monster, but that's another story.

Patrick Headland (11)
Threemilestone School, Truro

A Day In The Life Of A Groundling

(Based upon William Shakespeare and the theatre)

Dear Diary,

Ridiculous! Absolutely ridiculous. The actor dressed in long cut clothes prancing around like a fairy. I'm bored stiff, sitting here with my fruit and vegetables ready to throw any minute or grab his legs. I'm tempted. I'm like a stick in the mud all the way up to my knees. It's disgusting, absolutely horrendous. The rain didn't help. It's all slimy . . . hang on . . .

'You jaded, paper-faced, rabbit-sucker,' I shouted belting it out.

Honestly you come to see a play, you expect it to be good. Right that's it, I've had enough, I grabbed his legs and pulled him down. I think I did the boy a favour, he was making a right fool of himself. The crowd went wild. I mean . . .

'Ouch!' someone's just thrown a rotten tomato on my head. The crowds went mad. That's it! I'm on stage, thrashing everything, trying to fit in with the ones sitting in the galleries. Tomatoes, grapes, melons, you name it someone's thrown it. I feel all horrible and dirty. The clothes I've got on haven't been washed. I scrounge for money and search for food. I'm tired, hungry and really dirty. I live on the streets.

I have no home anymore. I have to steal to get into plays, just to get off the street. I have no family and no friends except the ones I steal and sleep with. I wish I had a miracle. Talk tomorrow.

Bye Diary
From John J.

Fiona Cunningham (13)
Whitburn CE School, Whitburn

A Day In The Life Of William Shakespeare

(Based upon William Shakespeare and his theatre)

Feeling very nervous on this play, as I lie in bed thinking of the worst, the best may happen. The play may be a success, or a failure. Is it to be or not to be, let's find out. The house is secure and I am thirty yards from The Globe. My emotions have the best of me. 'Five minutes gentlemen!' I shouted. 'You better be ready!' I shouted.

'We are!' they bellowed back.

'Well, let's do it now then!' I shouted.

They all hurtled from behind the curtain and some went on stage. The play had begun.

Forty minutes in and fire had struck the building. The place went up in flames and everybody got out. I felt so upset. I was devastated and annoyed at the rank, clay-brained rabbit-sucker that set it alight. The groundlings were going mad!

'We paid good money for this!'

'We want it back!' they all shouted.

Then one of the peasants threw a rotten tomato at me, so I ran home whilst on my tail were about fifty peasants throwing rotten fruit and vegetables.

When I got home they started throwing it at the house. So I sat in the house writing poems and plays. I was so bored. One couldn't think of anything else to do, so I looked outside and they were all gone, but I stayed in just in case they ambushed me.

So that's a day in the life of William Shakespeare.

Callum Jones (13)
Whitburn CE School, Whitburn

A Day In The Life Of A Groundling

(Based upon William Shakespeare and his theatre)

'Oh come on you lily-livered clot!'

God, I hate this play, it's one of the worst I've ever seen. You know what one of the actors in it called me earlier? He called me an onion-eyed rabbit sucker! Can you believe that? I'll have my revenge though, you can count on that. I have my bag of rotten tomatoes, oh yes, he'll be sorry. I'm not the one who needs to dress up as a woman on stage. I wouldn't come to see this play again mind you, it's awful. Absolutely terrible. I only come in to get off the streets in the first place, not to watch this rubbish.

'Boo hiss!' One shilling is a total disgrace if you ask me. It should be free . . .

'Hey, watch where yer throwin' those rotten tomatoes!' Stupid people who sit in the galleries, don't care who they hurt. It would be great to sit up there though.

'Come on God, please, once is all I ask.'

Oh it's no good praying. Instead, I just get shoved aside and trampled on like an insignificant other. Do people think I want to be poor? If I could choose my lifestyle, it would be the exact opposite, mark my words! Not that I'm greedy of course, but who would blame me if I was? My life's bad enough anyway.

Jonathan Tovey (13)
Whitburn CE School, Whitburn

Young Writers – That's Write! Write Up Your Street Vol I

83

Bewitched

Jayni had long glossy black hair down to her waist. Her face was thin and pale, she had mysterious emerald-green eyes that seemed able to penetrate people's minds and read their thoughts.

It was Saturday and Jayni was dreading moving house because that meant a new school. All of her furniture and possessions had been taken away. She sadly got in the car with her mum and dad, and stared out of the window at the pouring rain.

'Come on sweetheart,' her dad pleaded, 'it'll be alright when we get there.'

'No it won't, you know it won't,' Jayni replied.

The next day Jayni went to her grandma's house, and they looked at some old photos. Jayni flicked through the crinkled pages and saw a picture of a lady that looked like her.

'She's your great, great grandma,' her grandma said, pointing to the picture, 'she was a witch you know.'

Jayni left the house quickly after that. *My grandma must be crazy*, she thought, *there's no such thing as witches.*

The next day was Monday, which meant school.

At lunch one of the snobby girls called Amy came over to her and laughed, 'Oh, look here's a stupid, ugly nobody!'

Jayni stood up and glared at Amy with her magical eyes. Just then her dinner tray flew across the table and splattered bits of carrot all over Amy. *'You freak!'* yelled Amy as she ran away.

Jayni smiled and thought, *maybe there is something to witches after all, thanks Grandma.*

Claire Hutchinson (12)
Whitburn CE School, Whitburn

The Big Hungry Troll

One rainy, old, glum day in Dilston, there were three scamps of boys named Biv, Bov and Bav. The three 11-year-old boys were just sat down on a log next to their blazing campfire when a big tall man came walking towards them. At first the little boys were terrified but then when they realised he was trying to warn them about a big troll named Hogarth that lived under the bridge leading to the haunted castle, they were even more terrified.

The next day they had all forgotten about it and went to playing next to the bridge, they were all playing nicely until Bov tripped on a rock. Bav then picked up the rock and threw it towards the river.

Suddenly a great voice could be heard all around. 'Be, bi, bo, bum, I felt a block upon my nonce!' The big troll took Biv under the bridge and tied him up to a pole.

Meanwhile on ground level Bav and Biv thought up a master plan. The plan was to swing from each side of the bank one being a diversion so the other could grab Bov. They put the plan into action but as they swung, the beast saw them both coming, caught them and ate them, and then ate Biv. 'Oh what a satisfying meal that was,' said Hogarth the fat troll.

After that Hogarth went back to his ramshackled old hut and had a satisfying nap. The troll lived happily ever after.

Phillip Tedder (13)
Whitburn CE School, Whitburn

Young Writers – That's Write! Write Up Your Street Vol I

85

The Day My Life Had Changed

Dear Diary,

You're the only person that I can talk to, by the way I am Elle but you can call me Smelly Elle, everyone else does. I have no friends in my school class, and am always getting bullied because I wear glasses, it's silly really. They push me around thinking they're so big taking my dinner money.

I once plucked up courage to tell the teacher but they threatened me saying that if I did, I would never see the light of day again. But this was all about to change. It was Monday, this was the day that my life was going to change.

I was hiding away from the bullies so they wouldn't take my money, but I spoke too soon. Then I saw her, the girl, she had soft, silky hair and seemed perfect in every way, but I couldn't believe it, she wore glasses. I thought this girl was just another bully, and then she said it; the seven precious words to me, 'Hi, can I sit next to you?'

I tried to speak but nothing. I couldn't believe it, this perfect, popular girl was sitting next to me and she wore glasses, it was just so unbelievable. She started to talk to me more into the lesson and I soon found out her name, it's Hannah, she spoke in her soft and gentle voice. Hannah persuaded me to tell the teacher about the bullying.

Got to go, Hannah is calling for me.

Victoria Robson (13)
Whitburn CE School, Whitburn

The Return Of The Thing

(Year of Death)

It was a cold and miserable night. The wind whistled, the lightning flashed, and the thunder roared. It was the first day of the year 666. It was there in a small town known as Devil's Cove the thing that changed people's lives forever began. A brilliant red light appeared on the horizon. The terror it created lasted one whole year and throughout that year the sun was jet-black and the moon looked like thick red blood. Everyone hoped that this would never happen again . . . but they were wrong. In 1666, 1,000 years later it happened again.

It was 11.56pm 31st December 1659 and a 15-year-old boy named David's life was about to be changed forever because of what he saw this night. The church clock struck twelve bringing in the new year. On the way home a magnificent red flash caught his eye. He looked and watched as it emerged once more.

David fled in fear, unable to look at the thing. He ran to the hills and hid in the old, musty cobweb-filled mill. The only light that usually filled the sky was the stars. But tonight a flaming-being broke the darkness. David was crouching in fear, unable to move. It seemed to be circling him.

Now I leave you here . . . you can guess what happens to David. But remember it can only be killed by placing a gold cross over its head. Could you do it?

Gavin Catton (13)
Whitburn CE School, Whitburn

Young Writers – That's Write! Write Up Your Street Vol I

87

Space Ape

Jordon the ape lives in America. He loves space and dreams of visiting there one day.

One day Jordon was walking down the street and saw a poster in a shop window advertising a competition to win a trip to space. Jordon entered the competition and all he had to do was draw an ape. Jordon thought it would be easy. He sent in a photo of himself instead of a picture. Next day he received a letter saying he'd won the competition.

Excited Jordon was to be taken up to space in an hour. He quickly got some clothes and set off to the Space Academy. When he arrived he was excited to see pictures of space all over. The kind man in reception took Jordon to a big, beautiful spaceship; he met the crew who were to be on the spaceship with Jordon.

The journey began . . .

When Jordon arrived in space he was the first person off the spaceship. He was running around like a looney. It was not what Jordon was expecting but he was still excited to be there. After Jordon had calmed down he was feeling quite bored and he didn't like space anymore. Jordon decided to go for a walk and he bumped into a weird space dog called Pip, they had a game of fetch and then Jordon went back to the spaceship, but something was wrong, the spaceship and crew had gone.

Emma Dixon (13)
Whitburn CE School, Whitburn

The Griffin's Lunch

Once upon a time in 1385 only a few mythical creatures were left. There were two griffins. The mam was called Honey, the dad was called Grifolian. The mother went out to find some food when she got back, Grifolian said to Honey, 'Where did you get that from?'

Honey explained that she'd got it from over the hill in the village. Then suddenly a man sprang up over the hill and shouted, 'One day I will get you for killing my daughter and when I do everything you love will be mine,' and he galloped off.

Grifolian said anxiously, 'Let's get out of here.'

About nine months later Honey had two beautiful baby girls called Rose and Sunset. When they went out for their first flying lesson they saw a man galloping on a horse. They said, 'Mam what's he doing?'

She said, 'Run inside, I will sort this out.'

She went over to the man and shouted, *'Stop!* What do you want from us, we haven't done anything.'

The man said, 'You killed my daughter.'

Honey said, 'Why don't we work this out!'

He said, 'OK let's be friends then.'

The man walked away.

Grifolian said, 'We will eat him later.'

Paige Hall (12)
Whitburn CE School, Whitburn

A Day In The Life Of Elvis Aaron Presley

Elvis Presley came from a small town called Tupelo, Mississippi. It was on the edge of town that he first heard the blues.

His mother Grace Love Presley and his father Vernon Elvis Presley didn't have much money. They moved to a place called Memphis, Tennesse where he lived for the rest of his life.

For his mother's birthday he recorded a song at the local record shop called Sun Records owned by a man called Sam Phillips.

When he wiggled his hips and shook his legs on the Ed Sullivan Show, people were appalled but young Elvis never gave up.

At his first concert, a man named 'Colonel' Tom Parker went backstage to talk to Elvis who signed a contract to work with him.

By then Elvis had bought Graceland and was going into the army. He didn't realise that his mother was very ill. Elvis and his father visited his mother in hospital. His mother's eyes lit up but a couple of hours later she passed away and Elvis was left heartbroken.

In 1968, Elvis married Priscilla Beaulieu. A few years later Lisa-Marie Presley was born. Elvis was a very happy man.

He went on to make 30 movies, but Priscilla was missing Elvis and said that they should see other people. Elvis turned to drugs and gained weight.

His last concert would have been in Portville but he never made it. On August 16th 1977 the famous singer died in his home at Memphis, Tennesse.

Daniel Eisan (11)
Whitburn CE School, Whitburn

A Day In The Life Of Gladiator

I have been training extremely hard in a local area somewhere near Rome. It is a horrible and disgusting area. Everyone of us struggled to breathe!

My last fight (which was my first) I struggled with badly. However I feel I put on a good show as I was let off. From that battle, I received a serious injury and because of that, the Emperor, Augustus, has made me fight in the Colosseum.

This is why I have trained hard ever since my loss last week. I have now built my confidence right up, and I am unbeaten in the school, because of this I have received special armour from Phobos and Damos (the gods of war).

Tonight, I will be in the bloodthirsty Colosseum facing my toughest opponent yet. My opponent is believed to be unbeaten in 50 Colosseum fights! Although I am ready, full of confidence, bravery and pride. I worry. Today could be my last.

I feel nervous and confident as I walk towards the entrance of this beautiful arena. The Emperor, Augustus, has given me a dirty look as I enter the waiting room. The man before me has wet himself, he of course is worried more than anyone!

The door opened and I ran out, thousands of Roman citizens screamed at us. Some booed, some cheered. In front of us was 10 men waiting to dig their deadly weapons into our flesh.

Blair Adams (12)
Whitburn CE School, Whitburn

The Death Of A Legend

I am called Norma Jean Mortenson, I was born on June 1st, 1926 in Los Angeles General Hospital, my mother Gladys Monroe is mentally instable, I was never to know the true identity of my father, you may know me as Marilyn Monroe and this is my story.

There have been many reasons created why I died but nobody has ever known the real truth as to why I died.

Until now, it all started on the scene of 'There's No Business Like Show Business' the side effects of the many sleeping pills I had been taking for the last few years, I felt groggy, depressed, upset. I was ill with bronchitis and anaemia.

I woke up looking at Joe, we were to be divorced. He was still looking young and that terrible grin on his face was no more reassuring than being dangled over piranha-infested waters. He turned his back, I attempted to run, I knew this was trouble. I slowly edged off the end of the table, my feet and hands were roped! His henchmen picked me up, we were in a building I hadn't seen before, it was a warehouse, the walls were metal, the air was thick with smoke, a smell of old men filled the air.

They carried me to the car and locked the doors, Joe must have been getting his revenge, we were to be divorced later this year, we were moving to another location. The blood was racing through me, I couldn't breath, I was in shock and denial. Why would Joe do such a thing?

The speed of the car was picking up at an alarming . . . *watch out, car!*

Lauren Barras (12)
Whitburn CE School, Whitburn

A Day In Manchester

It was in the year 2003 and me, my dad, my mum and my uncle visited the Manchester United stadium called Old Trafford for a stadium tour.

We went to the main entrance and there were lots of people waiting to go on the tour. There was a man taking us around and he took us in the trophy room, the changing rooms and into the lounge where the players' wives/girlfriends sit when a match is being played. We took lots of photos and so did the other people.

At the end of the tour the man took us to the tunnel down on the pitch so that all of the people could run out onto the amazing Manchester United pitch. It looked great empty, and it looked like it was a bigger capacity than 67,000, it was more like 80,000.

After the tour I went to the shop under the stadium and bought a Manchester United top with van Nistelrooy and a number 10 on the back. Then after the Manchester United's stadium we went to Manchester City's stadium just for a look around. We took pictures there as well. We walked around the stadium and the shutters were open where the supporters come out, so we took some photos of the pitch.

After we left the stadium we went back to my uncle's, an hour away and then we went back home to Sunderland the day after. I am a Sunderland supporter but I like Manchester United too.

Dean Scrimgour (13)
Whitburn CE School, Whitburn

Hercules The Son Of Zeus

On one morning a baby called Hercules was born who was the son of Zeus. Hercules was a god so you could imagine how strong he was, he was a lot stronger than any ordinary man or woman. Hercules' father Zeus got him a flying horse called Pegasus so that when he became a hero if there was any trouble a long distance away he could get there quickly.

When Hercules got to ten he decided that he wanted to become a hero, like his father Zeus wanted him to become. So for Hercules to become a hero he would need a trainer. So Zeus told him where to get a trainer and that trainer was called Phil, but Phil said that he would never train another hero again, until he found out that Hercules had abnormal strength. Before Hercules could become a hero he had to do years of training.

When Hercules had trained for a couple of years he had to fight the most dangerous, fearful and unbelievable monsters to prove that he could become a hero and that he had enough courage and bravery to fight the scariest monsters. Also Hercules wasn't very easy to train because he was very clumsy so it took Phil a lot longer than he thought and it was a lot harder as well. But when Hercules did become a hero he could do some amazing things that even Achilles couldn't do.

Ellis Linney (12)
Whitburn CE School, Whitburn

The Magic Locket

One day at my grandmother's house she gave me a locket. My grandmother said that it was a very powerful gift, that I should look after it well. It had been passed down through the family and it was now my turn to have it. If I wore the locket and said or wished for something it would come true, but I had to be careful what I wished for, there would be consequences.

The next morning I put on the locket and went to school. All of my friends were crowding around me saying what a beautiful locket I had. They were bothering me a lot so at break I went into the girls' toilets and whispered very carefully into the locket for the first time and said, 'I wish people would stop bothering me.'

I went back into class after break and everyone was normal again, they didn't say a word about the locket. I thought to myself, *I guess it did work and it is a magic locket. This locket can change my life forever, I can get everything I want now.*

My teacher told us that we had a test in this lesson so I said to myself, 'Please let me do well,' over and over again. I felt really confident, and I flew through the paper.

I ran to my grandmother's house after school and thanked her again for the locket. I was very happy with the gift, and told her that I would use it well.

Danielle Ridley (13)
Whitburn CE School, Whitburn

My New Bed

Hi, my name's Lauren, I have two sisters called Lisa and Amy and my mum's called Tracy. I was down town when I saw it and I knew it was what I was dreaming about. There it was . . . a bed! It was sparkly silver with a lilac frilly quilt.

I had been sleeping on the floor for two months, so I went out and got a paper round and a job tidying gardens. My mum's disabled. She has to look after my little sisters. I help her out by giving her half of the money I make. I do my paper round every day and night then do some gardens. Me and my best friend Cheryl hang about on the merry-go-round.

After school me and Cheryl went to pay £33 for my bed. I was ever so happy. Cheryl was very proud of me.

My bed eventually came and it was very bouncy. Me, my sisters and Cheryl were bouncing on my bed and my mum started to cry. I went to see what was wrong with her. She thought she had let us down. We knew she hadn't. Then my sisters were upset about me having a new bed. I wasn't going to let them down so I gave up my bed and I ended up back on the floor with my mum.

Me and my mum snuggled in and went to sleep.

Lauren Jackson (13)
Whitburn CE School, Whitburn

My Lesson

My name is Becky and what I'm about to tell you is the most interesting and life changing thing that has ever happened to me.

It all started when I met a friend called . . . well I don't know what he's called but he is the friendliest, most caring person you will come across. He lives quite close to me, just at the back of that bus stop in front of my house. He lives alone and he never talks to anyone and no one ever talks to him except for the gangs of kids who shout and call him names. This man may only seem like an ordinary man to you, but you would change your mind if I told you this man was a tramp.

No I wasn't lying, when I said he lived behind the bus stop, he does, just next to the patch of grass that has been flattened where he has sat day in, day out.

This is where the lesson comes in, if I hadn't told you that he was a tramp would you have noticed or would you have just kept on thinking he was just an ordinary man? *No!* See he is an ordinary man, just without a proper home.

Everyone is the same, just because they live on the streets doesn't give anyone the right to shout and call names. Think about that, it definitely gave me a different point of view to life.

Becky Nellist (12)
Whitburn CE School, Whitburn

Prisoner Of War Escape

I heard two voices and then I slowly opened my eyes. Then I saw two German soldiers talking. After that one said, 'He's awake!' Where am I? Where is this place? Then all of a sudden they took a quick right and there in front of my eyes was a huge, gritty, old war prison with English prisoners. I thought, *I am going to die in here*. So I took one huge gulp of freedom's air and said, 'Goodbye freedom, you'll never see me again.' Then the next I knew I was getting dragged into the camp.

I just lay there on my bed thinking how to get out then it came to me. I could dig my way out.

'You get out of my bed,' said a short man, black with muck. I thought I was just going mad but then a hard object hit me on the face. I was back in reality.

After that I jumped up and off the bed. The rest of the day and night that bothered me, so I had to do it then but I was worried I could get caught and executed but I said to myself, 'I have the courage.' So from that moment on I planned my getaway. So then I tried to ease myself to sleep. The next day I dug for my life and then right that very second I was in freedom to live my life again.

Jamie Shotton (13)
Whitburn CE School, Whitburn

Day In The Life Of A Bullied Girl

It's 7am in the morning, I lay restless thinking of all the words that they could say to me like, 'Freak', 'mong', 'stupid', 'grasser' and 'liar'.

First lesson; it's getting too rough for me so I go to the toilets and talk to myself, I normally do this and it makes me feel much better.

I'm heading back now and feeling more confident to stand up for myself. As I step in the class I see one of the boys shouting at the teacher, he doesn't stop. He shouts at me, 'Here, look there's the freak coming in.'

I just hang my head in shame but it is not my fault, I've done nothing wrong.

Fifth lesson and it's still going on, one of the girls who is sitting in front of me says, 'Why do you grass all the time and why have you got no friends?'

I said, 'Well I do have friends and I probably have more than you!' Oh, what am I going to do? Then one of the boys comes over and he starts to push me over and over again until the teacher comes to see me.

She says, 'Are you alright Lisa?' and then turns to the boy and tells him to get out of the class.

When I get home I tell my mam what's happened and she says she will sort out this problem of mine so that my life can get better.

Nadine Helme (13)
Whitburn CE School, Whitburn

A Day In The Life Of A Teacher's Pencil

My teacher's pencil is sharpened and ready for work in his pocket by 8.55am. My teacher, Mr Lloyd's, pencil starts its working day. Lots of pupils in the class all need to be in registration. Names are called out and Mr Lloyd begins with his pencil. A tick if someone is present and a cross if someone is missing.

At 9.05am the pencil is put away until assembly is finished. Unless notes are needed during assembly.

The first lesson of the day and the pencil is taken from the pocket again. Not to write on the blackboard but to correct pupils' work either punctuation, capital letters etc, or even a tick if correct or a cross if wrong. If it's a cross then the teacher will write down the way it should be done.

By lunchtime it will probably have to be sharpened because by that time the pencil will normally have marked about 350 pupils' books. Perhaps even may have been re-sharpened at break time with marking so many books.

At lunchtime the pencil can have a well deserved 50 minute break. But at 1.25pm it all starts again.

Registration with a tick hopefully with the same people that were there in the morning. But then My Lloyd's pencil starts again marking with ticks and crosses and punctuation until the end of the day. 3.30 and it can finally finish with re-sharpening. Another day tomorrow.

Chris Prior (12)
Whitburn CE School, Whitburn

Fashion And Boys!

Once in the year 2004 two girls lived. The first Alex, 11 years old, the second Clair also 11 years old. All these girls wanted (and got) was fashion and boys!

One Monday it was just a normal, boring day at school for Alex but for Clair it was terrible . . . a huge spot, right between her eyes, smack-bang centre!

'What is that?' asked Alex.

'I know!' she continued, 'I'm going to have to cancel!'

'What?' Alex asked.

'Tonight, shopping, I'm going to have to cancel!'

'Oh OK, I can see why.'

So the day went by, the monster got bigger (the spot). At the end of the day it was the biggest spot they had ever seen! Clair pulled it, picked it and flicked it but still the spot did not get any smaller or come off.

The next day at school Clair and Alex walked round everywhere together when . . . they saw Mr Clark, the teacher they both fancied. Clair started pretending to scratch her nose (to cover her spot).

He looked, smiled and said, 'Hello girls!'

They just smiled and giggled a bit more than they were before he even spoke to them.

The bell went and the two girls walked off with a big group of boys. They went to first lesson and sat down on their wooden stools in the science room, then they began working till the second bell went. As the day went on the spot was noticed by more and more people. By last lesson the spot fell off and that's where the spot monster was made . . .

Lorna Gibson (12)
Whitburn CE School, Whitburn

The Time When Llamas Went Away

One fine spring day Egbert and Borris the llamas were dozing around in their field, eating grass and spitting at butterflies when they got bored.

They started to swim around in long grass and unknowingly, trampling on tiny bugs whilst they nibbled at their feet.

'Hey Borris, what's that little rabbit doing in 'our' field?'

'I couldn't tell you Egbert, just kick him away!'

'Oh you, what are you kicking that genie rabbit out of his field for? Not that it hurts or anything!'

This genie claimed that he would have granted the two llamas three wishes between them. But seeing as though they kicked him, he didn't. So they decided to apologise to the rabbit.

As they said sorry he gave them three wishes.

The llamas were overjoyed and thanked the rabbit. 'I wish for a year's supply of grass,' wished Borris.

'I want to be a giant llama,' said Egbert, 'so I can pick on Borris.'

'We wish for 'zebrahipadipalons' to arrive here in Llamaland!'

All of their wishes were granted, Borris got his grass, Egbert got his growth spurt and they both got a zebrahipadipalon. It was a magical animal; half zebra, half hippo with wings on its body. They jumped on the creature, as it was so big, and flew away just as the sun was setting.

Matthew Sampson Barnes (12)
Whitburn CE School, Whitburn

The Cursed Egyptian Queen

Long, long ago in Egypt, there was a man, he was the pharaoh of Egypt. His name was Seth II. Seth was a rich, evil man, the only thing to make him happy was to marry a rich girl. He looked at all the rich families in Egypt.

One day he came to a large, rich house. He walked in . . . he saw a slave, the slave bowed. 'Where is the owner?' Seth said.

'This way please,' the slave said.

'Pharaoh Seth! What are you doing here?' said Lord Memnam surprised.

'I'm looking for a wife! Do you have any daughters?' he said.

'Yes I do, I've got five. Nafito, Nemle, Shalee, Nafititi and Renchell,' boasted Lord Memnam.

'Who's best?' Seth said suddenly.

'Nafititi,' replied Memnam.

After that Nafititi was queen, she had long black hair, a crown and lots of jewels.

One day a snake came up to her.

'Help! What are you?' said Nafititi.

'A snake Your Hignessss!' said the snake.

'Hate the king, kill him and fall in love with High Priest of RA,' Ekankss said.

'I will,' said Nafititi.

One day she saw the priest and they kissed and they fell in love. Then she asked the king to come in her room.

'Kill him today,' said Ekankss.

'Yes Master,' Nafititi said.

When the pharaoh came in he kissed her and when he turned to leave she stabbed him. The guards heard him scream in agony and came in. After that Nafititi killed herself.

Ailsa Lilley
Whitburn CE School, Whitburn

Young Writers – That's Write! Write Up Your Street Vol I

103

Brain Storm

'Why do I have to wear pink?' I shrieked. 'It so doesn't suit me and I hate it! Please can I not just wear purple?'

'No! Pink is in, purple is out,' said Christie as if she was a fashion expert, which I suppose she is.

We were in the middle of a make-over at my house.

'Y'know there must be something wrong with your brain, pink totally suits you.'

That's when it struck me, that feeling as if someone was stabbing me in the back of my head. I've been getting it for ages now, but never told anyone, just kept it to myself I guess.

That night in bed I couldn't get to sleep. I was so scared as it was stormy and windy. Suddenly everything went really eerie and colder than it already was. Out of the blue six shiny white faces appeared. They had no eyes and blood around their noses. Then I noticed the scars in the exact place where I get my pains. One screamed. I was shaking with fear, I was trying to scream but I couldn't.

'You have our brains! You stole them in your previous life! You killed us for fun, give them back!' they screeched.

I yelped, *'Take them!'*

As quick as a flash they were gone. I ran to my mum's room, she did not believe me when I told her. You know it is true, or maybe you don't believe me. You should or something terrible may happen to you.

Sarah Duncan (11)
Whitburn CE School, Whitburn

Asylum

Doctor Rainfield walked through the gates of a large building named 'Greenfield Asylum for the mentally disturbed'. He unlocked the door and walked towards the desk. 'Morning Lenny,' he said.

'Same to you Sir,' said a red-haired guard. 'Mr Demonwarp wants to see you again.'

Doctor Rainfield stopped, then nodded. Demonwarp wasn't like any of the other lunatics, he kept his cool.

Richard Demonwarp looked at his cold macaroni and nibbled at it. Suddenly he became very serious. 'I want to talk about my inner demon,' he whispered.

'I see. What does he want?' the doctor asked.

'He wants me to do things that I don't want to do, like killing people,' he replied.

The doctor frowned. He wasn't usually like this. Most of the time he just wanted a small chat. 'I'll turn on the lights then, just to . . . '

'No!' He looked wild. 'Because then I could see him too!' He descended into screams about him dying. The doctor left.

He returned a few days later. As his ravings became more wild, he appointed a guard to watch him.

At home Dr Rainfield looked at his notes and tried to figure them out. Demons, hosts, only one day left till he dies. 'Hmmmm . . .' he wondered. He looked up mythical legends and old books. He found what he was looking for in 'The Book Of Evil'.

This account was written by David Lenny on the 21st of January, after Rainfield went insane. His patient died mysteriously two years later.

David Shiel (11)
Whitburn CE School, Whitburn

The Life Of The One And Only Marilyn Monroe

Is it the truth or has it been passed on? I guess nobody really knows. Can you imagine a day in the life of Norma Jean Baker (Marilyn Monroe)?

Forty-two years after her death and she is loved more than ever. She died at the age of thirty-six on the fifth of August 1962. Why did she do such a thing to herself? She must have been so fed up to do this. I assume that the truth is still out there, still looking to be found. She could have had a much longer life but she didn't.

She killed herself with a mixture of sleeping pills and whisky. Fair enough she got to sleep, but the fact is she never woke up.

Everyone thought she lived a wonderful life in sunny California then in the spotlight of Hollywood, but it seems as though it wasn't that great!

So I am writing today on the 24th of March 2004. Now everyone has heard of the one and only Marilyn Monroe, but why all of this publicity now when she is not here to live and appreciate it?

So can you imagine a day in the life of Marilyn Monroe? I know I couldn't, because after all she had to have had an awful life, so just think, what would you do if you just happened to be there, in her Californian home on the fifth of August 1962 when she committed suicide?

Samantha Kerr (12)
Whitburn CE School, Whitburn

A Day In The Life Of A Worm

'Just drop off your uncle's present and come straight home,' said Mum.

'I know, I know, bye!' I shouted. I was so happy that I was finally going to see my uncle! The grass tickled my sides as I squirmed through it and I passed many of my school friends on the way.

I had been travelling for about two minutes now and I knew that I would be there soon. Five minutes passed. Ten minutes passed and I still wasn't anywhere near my uncle's house. 'I must have gone the wrong way,' I said to myself and started retracing my steps. I finally realised where I was but then I heard something in the sky above. As I looked up, I saw a bird soaring through the air towards me.

Quick! Where could I hide? I knew that the bird could easily get me if I just stayed in the grass so I quickly dug my way into the ground. My heart was racing! I couldn't believe I had just escaped from being the bird's lunch! Quickly, I got back to my journey. I knew Mum would start to worry if I was any longer.

After passing some more of my school friends, I eventually reached my uncle's house. He was delighted when I handed him his present and because I was a bit frightened to go home by myself, I rang my mum and said that I was staying the night at my uncle's.

Kate Shaw (12)
Whitburn CE School, Whitburn

The Magic War

Two fairies called Georgia and Eve were playing the popular game 'Let's Beat Your Creature'. It was a game where you used magic to create a creature when the opposite team does the same and finally they battle and whoever's creature wins, the team get a point. As they were doing this the Wicked Witch and the Wacky Wizard were having an argument about whose turn it was to change the weather. But suddenly their angry faces changed into a huge smirk as they saw the two fairies. *The perfect dinner*, they both thought, mouths beginning to drool. In a flash of magic they were on their brooms flying across the spooky woods.

Meanwhile the poor fairies didn't have a clue what was going on as the sky started turning black, then green, then blue, then black again. Of course this was the witch and the wizard's happiness and what other fairies would class as a warning sign; but Eve and Georgia hadn't been in the town very long so just sat in a tree for shelter of the multicoloured rain beating against the ground like paint being splattered across a piece of paper. Now the evilness approached the witch and wizard again as they lost sight of the fairies so they flew back to their castle to find something else to argue about; and the two fairies finished their game off as the sun started to shine! Just an ordinary day in Silverton Land!

Eve Brown (11)
Whitburn CE School, Whitburn

Spook

It was a dark, windy night when Hannie the spook hunter went to Banakushka Manor, there was a strike of lightning as she knocked on the gloomy door which was opened by Barbie, a tall, glamorous witch.

'Oh hello darling, do come in for a cup of tea,' she said, as she pulled Hannie inside and into a bright pink sitting room.

A small white creature scuttled along, 'Rara,' it squeaked.

'Let me introduce my family, this is Bob,' she said pointing to a large man sitting on the sofa. He smiled showing two gleaming fangs, 'and this is RaRa our baby werewolf.'

Hannie introduced herself as a spook hunter.

Barbie was very pleased at this, saying, 'I'm glad you came, we have some very annoying spooks upstairs who we need to be rid of.'

'I will need to have a look,' said Hannie and the two women went upstairs.

A few hours later they all sat down for dinner. 'Obbeldy, gobbeldy, we want food! Food ghosts and spirits bring it to us!' Bob chanted.

'Raaaar!' squealed RaRa.

Bang! On the table was every food you could think of.

'Let's say grace,' he shouted merrily. 'Thank you God for sending Hannie, I hope we enjoy her. Thank you for . . . '

'*What?*' Hannie exclaimed. 'You're going to eat me?'

'No, no,' Barbie laughed, waving her hand. 'We hope we enjoy having you here!'

After that they started chatting away. 'So, you came here to kill us?'

'Well, it's a long story . . .'

Faye Bulley (12)
Whitburn CE School, Whitburn

A Day In The Life Of Electronorte (The World's Deadliest, Power-Hungry, Corrupt, Four-Times Running Chess Champion Of The World, Dam-Building, Rainforest-Destroying Vegetarian Darlik)

6.45am - Electronorte removes himself from his recharging device and wakes up to a hot cup of oil and some Netto Smart Price Quorn Flakes.

7.30am - Electronorte decides he needs a shower so he heads to the local rubber tree to get coated in delicious latex.

8am - Electronorte heads to Brazilia on his jumbo jet which has been carved from Brazil's finest hardwoods such as mahogany.

9.55am - Electronorte goes off to badger some Brazilian officials about using hydro-electric dams to power the Chinese war machine.

1.30pm - Electronorte has his hard-earned break from threatening Conservatives with weapons, carved from Brazil's finest animals such as spider monkeys, about burning the rainforest for fun. Today he has decided to go around mugging old people.

2pm - After discovering that the entire Brazilian government have run up a flight of stairs, Electronorte must go home early.

3.30pm - Electronorte arrives home to his hydro-electric dam in the Amazon.

3.45pm - Electronorte beats his hamster at chess for the 51,397,206th time.

4.30pm - Electronorte loses the annual 'How much of the rainforest can you destroy a year?' competition to the Thailand Destroyer.

4.35pm - Electronorte goes out to zap some spider monkeys.

5.55pm - Electronorte works on his plan to transport Sunderland to the rainforest so the youths can start to burn down the rainforest for fun before going back to his recharger.

Jamie Anderson (13)
Whitburn CE School, Whitburn

A Day In The Life Of My Mum

Here I am, in English. We have just been told that we need to write a short story about someone famous who we think is an inspiration to us all. Obviously, the usual David Beckham, Britney Spears and Blazin' Squad are the main favourites, with Michael Jackson, quite disturbingly, also being written about. My mind goes blank. Then I thought to myself, *Do you have to be famous to be an inspiration?*

I looked to my friends. My teachers. My family. That bloke that gets the bus every morning. Then I thought of my mum. Maybe not the best, most famous, beautiful or cleverest person in the world, but the most inspirational to me.

My mum wakes up. Or rather she is still awake from worry. There is nothing in particular to worry about, but she always has this amazing ability to find anything to lose sleep over. She has to wait half an hour whilst I use the bathroom, making her later than she usually is. She gets in the car, but on the way to work her car breaks down because the battery has gone. We have never had any luck with cars. We have had about 10 different ones in the past year. If there was something that could go wrong with them, it always would.

My mum's new job brings her so much happiness, she has become a teacher teaching people with learning difficulties. It can be a bit risky though, as sometimes no one turns up or her courses are cancelled. She works hard to plan her lessons, but for whatever reason, if the pupils don't turn up, those hours of hard working are gone, for 15 minutes of picture books and slide shows.

After skipping lunch she trails to another job which she has to go to to get enough money to support us.

She goes from work to my grandparents' house where she checks on both of them to see if they are still well or if my disabled grandma is still ill from her never-ending injections she has and the thousands of fist-sized tablets she is forced to take every day just to try and stay alive.

My mum then comes home, tired, hungry and crying, faced with me shouting and blaring because she is five minutes late and forgot to get my pocket money from my grandad because she was too busy spoon-feeding my grandma. I am in a rage because I fell out with someone at school for scribbling on my pencil and now I hate how my mum is always miserable.

She staggers upstairs trying to ignore the abuse that I give her, expecting my father to come galloping in on his white horse after he left her with me when I was a child, alone and forever. She stumbles and falls on a pile of brown, bill-like envelopes saying *'urgent'* and *'important'*. She crawls to her bedside and clambers into bed.

The clock says 12.51 and she weeps as she thinks how much better she could have made her life. The house is in entire darkness and she switches on the light to see if she can grab a glass of water, her only food all day, but she finds the light bulb is still dead, as it has been for the past six years, but because Dad fitted it, it resembles him and we must hold onto it.

She then gets to the kitchen and finds a flower on the table with a note beside it. It is addressed from Laura. She reads it. 'Dear Mummy, I saw this and thought of you. I know you love daffodils, and so did Daddy, but this is for you, I picked it from the front garden'. The front garden was full of weeds and rubble from the tumble-down wall of our neighbours. I did try to clean it up every now and again, but it was impossible, the more you looked, the more rubbish and dirt there was. 'Amongst all the weeds, I found this, the ray of sunshine and beauty that I only thought existed in fairy tales. It is magical, and true, like ice, like fire, the harmony of its clean-cut, yellow petals lying gently on the grass-green stem, full of laughter and light. This reminds me of you, and how you are, with deep beauty inside, yet you can never let it out. Through all the grime and dust, you arise with deep beauty and kindness, against all odds, surviving on the tip of water your most feeble, weak root can reach, gently growing more and more beautiful each day. Hold this close to your heart, and with it think of yourself - no one else - and what the future has to hold. The daffodil will be your inner guidance and it will tell you how I love you'.

I sit under the stars, wondering what the future will hold, with the most chilling silence of care through my mind. The wind gently whistles through my hair. It was a wonderful, starry night. My mum stands behind me.

'It is amazing that the beauty of the stars is always there, yet has the ability to be blocked by the mist and clouds of the sky. Someone once told me that the stars are the father of your fate. The mother is your own soul. What do your stars say?'

'The clouds are in front of mine,' I reply. 'What do yours tell you?'

'Mine are the clearest they have ever been. They are filled with colour and prospect. But tonight, my soul is the clearest it has ever been.'

'What does it say?'

'It tells me that I am lucky to be a part of this world. It tells me that I am lucky that someone loves me. That brings me the happiness of the world. This is my soul. As it always has been, just the mist took a long time to clear.

My mum is not David Beckham, Britney Spears, not Michael Jackson or even a member of Blazin' Squad. She is not the best, most famous, beautiful or the cleverest person in the world, but the most inspirational to me. And for that, I have chosen to write about her today.

Laura Young (13)
Whitburn CE School, Whitburn

A Day In The Life Of A Lawnmower

I'm sitting in the shed now and I haven't been used for ages. It must have been three months since I've been used. I hope Mr Bob hasn't forgotten about me . . . wait! I hear somebody . . . *argh*! The light, it burns! Yey, Mr Bob is here! And with food/petrol.

But I'm not petrol powered, I'm electrical. What's that? Oh no! Mr Bob has got a new lawnmower. This can't be happening to me. *Nooo!* He will regret buying that lawnmower. I'll kill him! No, even better I'll murder the new lawnmower. I'll get in the dark, I'll plug myself in and scrap its shell off. It will get so cold it will not ignite and get chucked out! Ha ha ha!

Hey! I'm being moved. Wait. It's Mr Bob he's going to chuck me out. Please don't do it! Huh! I'm going to the scrapyard. No! Don't chuck me, *bang! Ouch!* Mr Bob's bullying me. How could he do this?

Wow! We're moving. It's quite smooth. *Argh!* I've fallen off the seat. I'm useless now. I don't think I've served my master well. I deserve to be chucked out. I'm here now. I wonder what they'll do to me now? Goodbye Mr Bob.

Wow, I'm flying! Clunk! Ouch my head. It's the big magnet thing. It picked me up and . . . *argh!* I'm falling! *Bang! Ow!* I feel like a cabbage drowning. I don't have the strength to fight myself out of a wet paper bag now. I've lost my wheels and lost half of my shell.

Who are they? I hope they're nice to me. They're picking me up and *Argh! Ow!* They are nasty passers-by. They are . . . charves. Save me dear God. Please. *Ugh!* I see the light. Heaven is opening up to me. I must be dead.

Scott Bullock (12)
Whitburn CE School, Whitburn

A Day In The Life Of Mary

I feel quite lost. Everyone will be upset. I was told today . . . I have breast cancer. I don't know how to tell anyone. I'm scared. Not of death but of the torment that will pursue. My family were upset when I was first brought into hospital. I don't know how they'll take my death. They're coming here later. They always visit.

The family arrived, the girls as well, they're getting older and they all seemed so quiet! I wish they knew. I don't want them to be told last. I told my daughters though, and dear Bill, he already knew. If there would be one thing I could change it would be we would go together. He's probably going to have to celebrate our anniversary alone. I don't think I'll be with him. I will actually. I will exist. But only in his heart. I wonder how he must feel. I'm growing weaker throughout the day.

I can barely hold the pen. This is my last diary entry. I will go now. Forever. I love you all, my family. Dearest family.

Hannah Robson (13)
Whitburn CE School, Whitburn

The Mellowship Of The Toe Ring

'Welcome to The Wire', it says as you walk, run or travel on public transport as you come into the border of The Wire. A small place where large Snobbits walk around freely and small human wizards don't. Anyway back to the plot. Grandalf, a human wizard, was out on his daily shop for toilet rolls, when he saw a terrible sight, a terrible sight it was, Charles, you know the one from the chocolate factory, and his mate, Rolled Dalf, were walking down the same aisle. They are ill-mannered people and shouldn't be allowed in The Wire. They vandalise hills and everything like that. So, they were in the same aisle as Grandalf. They walked past, they did nothing, Grandalf thought something was wrong. Although he did smell a horrible smell, a horrible smell of dried grapefruit, a terrible smell in The Wire, I do say. Grandalf caught sight of a small envelope they were carrying. *Their strangeness must have something to do with that envelope,* Grandalf thought. *I'd better not do anything because I might end up on one of those crazy adventures from that book I read,* he thought in a carrying on manner.

When Grandalf got home he put his bags of toilet rolls on the floor, and went to his sofa to have a rest, when suddenly . . . there was a knock on the door. He opened it, was it the butcher? No, was it the neighbour? No, of course, it was Brodo, the wise, very tall person. he was holding something in his hand. Grandalf had a confused look on his face as if he wasn't sure what was in his hand because Brodo had enormous hands.

'Hey-o,' Brodo said, in an insane manner.

'Hi, what do *you* want?' Grandalf replied.

'Here, have this.' Then he ran away.

Grandalf held it in his hands. It was the envelope from the shop, the one that the horrible people were carrying.

The envelope started to light up. It spun above Grandalf's head, and cut some of his hat off. 'Ow!' The envelope started to burn a bright blue. The envelope burned away into ashes onto the ground, and then disappeared, and there in Grandalf's hand lay The Toe Ring. There are myths about The Toe Ring, but Grandalf thought they were a load of lies. There he held the most powerful toe ring, and this isn't in general.

Ten minutes later Grandalf was still in the same position, staring at it in shock. When he actually got out of his state of shock, he noticed a note on the floor. He picked it up. It read 'Destroy the toe ring in the centre of the Hill of Doom'.

Again Grandalf stood there for ten minutes in shock, but then he thought it was silly, so he went to bed.

The next day Grandalf thought about the quest afoot, and decided to make a crack team. So he went about The Wire in search of a perfect team. The first person he decided to pick was Brodo, after all, he was the one with all the information. He's his own information booth! The second person he picked was Scam, an Irish bloke with scanning powers, his name fits with it, and last of all Terry the Trumpeter. He is sure to bring some entertainment.

So they set off to get some food and drink for the journey. Down the path they went, Terry playing the trumpet and they all marched. This makes people walk in a rhythmic action. So they missed all the action (damn, less writing for the writer. Awww).

'Ahhh,' shouted Grandalf, 'who is that following us?'

Brodo replied in an informational manner, 'It's Smurfil! He is one of the followers of The Toe Ring. He can't do anything. We'll just prod him down the hill in an orderly manner.' So they carried on talking and enjoying the trumpeting when they came to the mountain.

'Do we really have to climb this mountain, Brodo?' Terry the trumpeter said in a moaning way.

'No,' Brodo said.

'Is that all you're going to say?' Grandalf added.

'Yes, just follow me,' Brodo said, in a way of a follow-me-manner.

They followed Brodo and ended up at a wall. There was an inscription on the wall. It read 'Speak friend and you may pass'.

'It's a riddle,' Terry said inconspicuously.

'Friend!' Grandalf shouted.

The door opened, and they missed the monster because of the rhythmic marching. (C'mon Terry the Trumpeter!) They all walked in. Brodo lit up his magic fish. Very light it was. There was a load of forks lying around. They all stared in a confused way. Ten minutes later they all picked up a fork and went up the stairs. There were many more forks. At the top of the stairs they came across a large novelty door. They opened it and it started shouting Internet adverts out. Very strange! Inside the room there was nothing, nothing at all, until they all fell down trapdoors and went down the water slides.

'Wheee,' they shouted in glee.

At the bottom they ended up on the other side or the mountain. They thought it was so easy so they went back around, but they were held up, there were queues for the slides. So they decided to walk around the mountain, which took half the time, but less fun. At the other side there were fields and small patches of forestry, with people in wheelchairs spinning around. They all decided to avoid all the wheelchairs. It took them 87 years to cross the big field, but thanks to anti-ageing cream they stayed the same and didn't age at all, and had the same fitness from running for 87 years. Unfortunately Terry the Trumpeter died, from no gas syndrome, but to keep their amusement up they pushed along a spinning weirdo. Very amusing.

Then they came to a forest, a large forest. They say that the only way to get to the Hill of Doom is by the river, which is in the middle. In the 87 years that they had been adventuring they found out that the forks were actually dead Klorks. They are deadly beasts powered by the magical Coco Pops. They will have to be on the lookout for these beasts.

35 years later the main action of this adventure happened. The Klorks came from behind, but luckily the abnormal person used to be a ninja before he became a full time abnormal person so he got out of his wheelchair and started to attack them, and also a handy thing, the Klorks that turned into forks made good cutlery for their dinner.

They decided to walk faster because they smelled that they were close.

25 minutes later they heard water. They heard water, and fantastically a ferry was there. They paid with Grandalf's toilet rolls he conveniently had in his pocket.

The fellowship continues in the next book.

Daniel Bates (13)
Whitburn CE School, Whitburn

A Day In The Life Of Louise

I woke up, still shaking from the night before. I still can't believe what happened. Maybe it was a dream . . .

It started just like any other day. I woke up with the hot, blazing sun beating down on me, heating my skin. My children were already awake and had left for the grassy patch where they could play safely in the shade of the weeds. I looked around me and saw that the sand was bone dry. The small amount of hope that I had left drained away leaving an empty space inside of my heart. We were going to go another day without water.

Suddenly, all of my senses came flooding back to me like a tidal wave as I heard a loud bang in the distance. A few birds came swooping out of a nearby tree shouting, 'They got Summer! Louise, they got Summer!'

'Who's got Summer? Who?' But no sooner had I asked that two strange creatures that I'd never seen before came out of the bush. They were tall with no fur except for a small amount on their heads and they stood on their hind legs. One of them carried a long silver tube with smoke coming out of the end. I'd heard of these things before. It was a gun. The other one was carrying a silver cage with a bundle of orange and black stripy fur in it, it was Summer, my daughter. I came bounding out from behind the tree, growling as loud as I could. The creature with Summer dropped the cage and it sprang open. She ran, stumbling, back into the grass. She was safe. The creature ran away. The other one shot three things out of the gun, hitting me in the leg and paw. He ran off after the first.

My leg was bleeding and I collapsed onto the warm soft sand. We had a lucky escape, but something was telling me that those two-legged animals would soon be back to try and get us again . . .

. . . after all, tiger skin is very valuable.

Stephanie Lee Mart (14)
Whitburn CE School, Whitburn

A Day In the Life Of A Child During World War II

'The Germans,' I whispered under my breath as the siren for *attack* sounded. The name echoed in my head, and my heart began to beat faster and faster inside my thin, pale chest. The word was not to be said as it would create worry and tension in the underground tunnel most of our townspeople were sheltering in. The tunnel sheltered us from the horrific sights of our fathers, uncles and elder brothers in battle to defend our country, Britain, from the aggressive and terrifying Germans.

I was just one of a handful of children who were nuzzled into their mother's chest for comfort and safety; the Germans had sunk the remains of the passenger ships to and from safer towns and countryside, so I was not one of the evacuees who had to go and live in the middle of nowhere, away from their worried families. There must have been around 300 tired, worried and distressed people nestled in blankets and drinking tasteless tea and eating watery cabbage soup. Our rations had nearly run out, and we were sick of the same cabbage-flavoured water and steaming tea which burnt the roof of my mouth each time I took a cautioned sip.

Oh how I missed my friend Elsa, who had been shipped off three weeks ago to live in the heart of Yorkshire, surrounded by beautiful hills and fluffy white sheep. I wondered if she was missing me too. She wrote to me once, when she arrived in a large manor house with a tall, tight-lipped woman named Mrs Jenkins, and a ferocious tabby cat named Precious. I could not wait until we had defeated the awful Germans, and this wretched war was over so I could see Elsa, and have my lovely, funny father back home. But at least I had my mother. I loved her so much, and I knew we could get through this together, and finally see my brave father who had volunteered to fight for his country.

As I snuggled into my mother's plump chest, I sniffed her sweet, musky scent, and held her slim, delicate hand. It seemed cold, and her veins had become blue, and very prominent. As I slowly looked up at her shapely, normally rosy and smily face, she seemed in a trance. Her beautiful blue eyes were startled and wide open. They were unblinking, her black lashes, and perfect eyebrows were still. I began to shake her. I knew there was something wrong.

'Mother . . . Mother!' I shouted as our inmates began to dash towards us. My mother's hand slipped from mine and thudded on the dirty stone floor as her head lolled against the wall. She looked like a pale china doll. She was beautiful.

I continuously shook my mother, and my desperate shouts turned into screams. How could this happen? She was my kind and loving mother, and now she had left me on my own. What was I going to do? I hung my head, as cold tears rolled down my face, and I slowly put my arms around her neck and hugged her as her beautiful soul drifted up to Heaven.

Anna Moutafis (14)
Whitburn CE School, Whitburn

A Day In The Life Of A Sloth

I'm sick and tired of being called lazy! It's a busy and hectic life being a sloth, it's just I can't run very fast. Lots of humans can't but I don't point and laugh at them! The baboon in the next cage says I'm being touchy; the nerve! He's the one who was complaining last week because some humans were laughing at him when he turned around. He's a little too sensitive about that particular area.

I'll prove those humans wrong one day. I'll move more than fast, more like lightning! They'll all stand there gaping like they do at the tiger, he gets far too much credit for an animal, and rush to buy posters of me for a change!

I'm just as interesting as those stupid seals! They balance a ball on their nose and the crowd goes wild! Well I can find leaves at the tops of huge trees and have really big claws, if I do say so myself. OK they might not be as pretty as a striped coat or a big mane but they're very practical. All I want is a little credit.

Oh look, more humans, surprise surprise they're laughing at me and . . . look! That man's put his fingers into *my* cage! Right, when I get over there he's in so much trouble! OK left hand, swing, now right hand, swing, just wait. Left . . . right . . . left . . . right and . . . wait! Walking away now are we? Yeah, should think so too!

Humans. They act tough but really I'm king of the jungle!

Joanne Rossiter (13)
Whitburn CE School, Whitburn

A Day In The Life Of A Child In The War Time

The rumbling of my stomach woke me; another long boring day lay ahead.

I didn't like this new way of life. People seemed different, like they didn't care as much anymore, or that they have something very serious on their mind yet still refuse to share it. Like there's something to hide. When I ask my mum would always say, 'You're too young' or 'go and play'. she couldn't tell me where my dad was and when I questioned her she simply turned away as her eyes filled up. She thinks I don't notice.

Each day was the same. I would wake up and venture downstairs to find my mum and Auntie Linda whispered over their cups of tea; abruptly they would raise their voices with a completely different subject.

I dreaded school. The other children got less playful and more spiteful. I often found myself on my own at playtime. Why was the sudden change? I waited anxiously for the bell to ring. The minutes seemed like hours. Each and every day I rushed home hoping to see my dad sitting there reading the Daily Mail on his chair. I was beginning to lose hope!

I wasn't allowed to play in the street. My mum was quite over-protective. For this particular night I was glad. I had a weird sensation in my stomach the night before, now I know why.

It was about 10.15. I was nearly asleep but kept awake by the voices next door. Unexpectedly, a strange siren went off. Like the ones we have in school when there is a fire drill. Only this time, it felt seriously worrying. I ran to the top of the landing to see Auntie Linda waiting. The look of panic on her face immediately made tears roll down my cheeks. Mr Gardener from next door swept me up into his arms and took me into the shelter in the garden.

It was dark and cold. We stayed there all night until a friendly face appeared and said, 'All clear.' That is definitely not something I would like to experience again, although my instinct tells me otherwise.

Carly Henderson
Whitburn CE School, Whitburn

Hello?

Jake was alive! He may have plunged into water from a 30 foot drop in complete darkness, but he still hung in there. Frantically swimming away from the rock face he scrambled for shore looking for help.

Ahead of him he saw a light, coming from a candle in a window, so he ventured up the hill in his soaked clothing to where it was coming from. Being cold, his pace was faster than usual.

Jake got to the window and peered in just as the candle burnt out.

'Hello?' he shouted, when he saw movement inside.

Soon after that a clash of pans or something or other came from the kitchen. There definitely was someone inside and they were trying to escape.

'I'm not here to hurt you,' Jake explained, 'it's just, well I've fallen. Have you got a phone, or even some spare clothing?'

Out of the distance came an old woman.

'Here,' she said, handing over a towel, 'I don't have any clothes but you can dry off with this.'

Jake smiled at her while he was drying off, it must have been the first smile she had seen in years as it brought a smile to her face as well.

By the faint light of the burnt out glowing candle he saw a red phone in the corner of the room.

'Can I use that?' he asked.

'Yes, but I don't know if it'll work as I haven't used it,' she replied.

Jake dialled home.

'Mum?'

Calum Dobson (13)
Whitburn CE School, Whitburn

The Siren Of Hell!

I woke up one summer's morning and had a look outside, the sun was shining brightly. I quickly got ready to catch the bus to school. When I got there, we were doing WWI in history. The soldiers whom I read about sounded brave; I couldn't stop thinking about them.

That night I was wondering about the life of a WWI soldier and how they must have felt, as I drifted deeply into the Land of Nod. That night the sound of a siren awoke me, as I opened my eyes everything seemed different, I wasn't in my room.

I stood up and looked around me, there were men; all dressed in camouflage, they were covered in blood and mud, you could see the fear in their eyes, I began to panic.

'Second platoon,' a deep voice shouted. I felt a push and followed a small group of men.

As I followed them we ended up running across a muddy field; bullets were flying and bombs going off, dead men were lying on the ground covered in lice. My heart was racing. I felt a sudden pain in my side; I looked down at myself and I was covered in blood. I was in a hospital; the nurses were referring to me as the lieutenant. I was scared.

I closed my eyes and as I opened them I was back in my bed. I was so glad to be home. Now I know how brave the soldiers really were.

Kirsty Rodgers (14)
Whitburn CE School, Whitburn

A Day In The Life Of A Soldier

The trench was dark and had a foul odour that seemed to sting the back of your throat when you breathed. Not that the biggest of our worries was a funny-smelling trench. You would think that being in the middle of a war would make you ignore things like that; I have found it just makes me more aware of everything. It makes me more aware because I realise that this could be the last time I see the sides of the trench around me. This could be the last time I smell it, although I don't imagine the stench would be missed.

I realise there are two ways out of the war: win or die. The battle raging in front of me has not been the only one going on. I have been fighting a battle with myself constantly over which option I would rather have. I don't feel right out here. I haven't felt right since the very first day of this war, when I saw a man killed.

Killed by my own hand.

The bullet that I saw tear into him seemed to pierce my brain and I haven't been able to get the thought out of my mind ever since. Even in the darkness of the trench I see it, it haunts me. I shouldn't be out here. I don't want to fight. Why should I fight to save my country when I don't even want to save myself?

Rachael Walsh (14)
Whitburn CE School, Whitburn

A Day In The Life Of A Soldier

My name is James Murdoch, I'm nineteen years old. I'm a soldier. I have been for two years; shipped out to the front line a mere youngster greedy for action. But now, I just wish this war were over.

I dress in bog standard camouflage gear with mud-riddled hair and army paint smeared across my brow. Gun in hand; we listen to the sergeant bark orders through the damp, narrow gutters. It's no consolation to think we are fighting for king and country.

The trenches themselves are vile. Dirty, smelly and downright gloomy. They are infested with rats, crawling like swarms of ants over the dead, decaying bodies. Our wounded lie strewn across the battlefield, no one daring to rescue them fearing they are hit themselves.

As for the food: it's disgusting. A diet of stale bread and murky water can't be good for soldiers. Nevertheless, this depressing dwelling is home. Give me England any day, country roads, thick pine forests, and loving family around me.

Wake, watch, wait. Wake, watch, wait. That's all we ever did . . . until yesterday.

German bombs targeted us. Shrapnel flew everywhere. Men scattered, trying to keep a solid formation. It was impossible. A segment of metal whistled past my cheek, missing by millimetres.

I heard a heart-rending shriek from behind. The same piece of metal was wedged firmly in my friend's chest. I spun round to help him - but what could I do? I'm not a doctor. He died a slow and painful death.

Army life. It kills.

Rebecca Kranz (14)
Whitburn CE School, Whitburn

A Day In The Life Of Merlin The Cat (The Night Manoeuvres)

Merlin the cat was infamous around his neighbourhood. His nights were our days; while his human parents were at work you could trust Merlin to be asleep, probably in the washing basket! It puzzled him that every evening when his human mother arrived home he was rudely awakened, shouted at and plonked outside. However, he didn't really mind, he simply treated it as a free taxi ride to the front door.

Nothing was ever easy when it came to Merlin's night manoeuvres. Mr Wig lived next door and he hated cats. He was the owner of a 'Super Soaker 3000' which Merlin had been violently squirted with many times. Then there was Bruno, the Jack Russell, from No 31, and the night hadn't started yet!

After running for his life from Bruno he eventually found his gang, only to be distracted by a cheeky little brown mouse just asking to be caught, and of course Merlin obliged. The chase was on! Merlin raced after the mouse and left his gang far behind.

He pounced several times, but this mouse wasn't giving up that easily and he found himself in pursuit again. When at last he caught the mouse, he was feeling quite generous and took it home to his human parents as a kind of peace offering. They didn't seem to appreciate his gift and he watched as his freshly caught juicy mouse was set free, to add insult to injury he was presented with dry cat biscuits for breakfast. *Humans,* he thought, *are very strange!*

Amy Edmondson (13)
Whitburn CE School, Whitburn

A Day In The Life Of The Sun

Firstly, I don't measure time in days. How can I? Everywhere has their own clock and time difference; one day in one place is the day before in another. No, I have to measure time in years; how many times the Earth goes around me.

Being the sun has its perks: unlimited space, utmost respect and the chance to be 'the centre of the universe'. But, I have to admit, I do get lonely sometimes; I cannot have contact with anything, because I have - how should I say - a rather hot temper, and a short fuse.

I never sleep: there's always some country that wants it to be daytime, always someone that wants it to be summer - some countries demand more heat than others; Australia for example. They always want it to be sunny, and I am legally bound to comply. This means that smaller countries, such as England, don't get as much of my energy as I'd like them to get.

Because of me there is everything; I'm not being big headed, when I die, the rest of my area will die too. Sometimes I get so angry; there's very little for me to do, but watch everything ignoring me, taking me for granted. That's why I sometimes send out sparks (which humans call asteroids), as warnings. Doctors say it isn't good to keep your anger bottled up; but I have little option other than to sit fuming inside, biding my time.

Emma Noble (14)
Whitburn CE School, Whitburn

The Myth Of The Yeti

I sat up in bed and sighed. On first hearing I'd be coming to the Scottish Highlands for Easter, I'd screamed. The holidays, a time for sleeping and eating chocolate. Slowly, I climbed out of bed, peering out of the window. Miles of snow, snow and more snow! Looking at my watch, I saw it was 7.15. Too early.

After much squabbling, we were all ready for our first day of skiing. We set off, my baby sister Steph on my dad's back, my little sister Emily holding his hand. I was at the back, struggling with the weight of my skis and having to walk in ski boots.

At the top, my dad did his usual, 'if you get lost' speech, and then I was off. The 'I want to be home' thing disappeared as I flew down the slope, the wind in my hair. Looking around I saw a jump someone had made, so, bending my knees, I prepared to soar over it.

Ow! What I thought was a jump, turned out to be a stone. I lay there in the cold, my back aching. I turned over, ready to stand up, and saw a huge mark, a cross between a human footprint, and a dog's, except ten times bigger. Taking a sharp intake of breath, I closed my eyes and laughed. Yetis, Bigfoot, whatever you want to call them, are for story books.

I shook myself off, stood up and looked around. Disappearing into the woods behind me was a large, dark shape.

Lucy Walker (13)
Whitburn CE School, Whitburn

The Hand Of Glory

For centuries people have believed in various charms concerning dark magic and witchcraft. The Hand of Glory is said to be one of these magical charms. It is made from a mummified hangman's hand. This hand has been squeezed of all of its blood, fat and veins (which made the candle, that sits in the palm of the hand). This hand is said to render the surrounding people in to a state of unconscious sleep.

This hand was used by a band of robbers on an October's night in 1797. It was a cold, stormy night when George Anderson opened his inn doors to a hunched old woman. George Anderson, the innkeeper, lived with his 14-year-old son and maid, Bella. The old woman said she was travelling south but needed to retire for the evening due to the weather. The old woman refused to retire to a room, instead sitting by the fire.

Bella could not sleep that night with curiosity and worry about the strange old woman and her peculiar behaviour. Bella tiptoed downstairs, candle in hand to check on the old woman. To Bella's shock she did not find an old woman but a young, hard-looking man, unravelling himself from a bulky cloak; perching a grotesque-looking hand on the table.

The maid hurriedly dashed upstairs to wake George Anderson, but found she couldn't. Returning back downstairs she found the man in a trance, chanting words to the hand, 'Let those who rest more deeply sleep, let those awake their vigil keep. Oh Hand of Glory shed thy light, direct us to our spoil tonight.' Bella then doused the candle in milk. Moments later Mr Anderson and son came running down the stairs with gun in hand. The robbers soon fled, the inn's profits in hand, but were pulled to a halt by the shots of Mr Anderson's gun. Injured the robber said he would return the money for the Hand of Glory which had been left on the counter of the inn. Mr Anderson refused the robbers their Hand of Glory and returned to the inn, in fear of his son's safety. The Hand of Glory stayed at the inn for many years before mysteriously vanishing on a cold, stormy October's evening.

Imogen Nicholson (13)
Whitburn CE School, Whitburn

A Day In The Life Of A Soldier

We had been fighting for weeks now, even months, and I keep thinking to myself, *when is this horror going to stop?* I just want justice for my country and be able to go home and see my family.

My name is John Tawny, it has been my dream to be in the army, and I am currently fulfilling it. I have been in the army since I was 19 and I am soon approaching my 31st birthday. I am a Lance Corporal and I lead my troop of seven privates and myself. We are fighting in the Falklands War, against Argentina. The reason for this was Argentina had invaded and occupied the Falklands Islands, which Britain rightfully own. We sent over a British task force, and the war progressed from there.

I had originally started out with a troop of ten, but tragically two of my privates were killed in action. Those days were so tough, but I had to keep going and make sure no more lives were lost. Those days I could relive and tell the story word for word. Like one particular day, which set me back.

It was a bright day and the sun was gleaming. It made me feel happy and at home. But I knew it would be another day of torture. The tension and suspense whilst attacking is very fearful. You don't know whether you will fight again or if this will be your last fight. We got ready quickly and went out to join the rest of the troops to begin firing.

We went and took our positions around base. The sound of the opponents' gun shots were getting closer and closer. For a minute I doubted whether I would still live to tell this tale.

James, a private in my troop, was a very good friend. I had gone all the way through the army with him and I treated him like a brother. I always stayed with him and I felt safe being near him.

On the particular day, we ducked down further under the sandbags, lining out the trench. We tried to camouflage ourselves but we knew it would be no good. For the first time ever, I could see the fear in James' eyes. But in my mind, I was just as scared. We loaded our guns so they were ready to aim and fire, as we had no intentions of giving up and surrendering. We had been in this war for a long time now, we weren't going to give up.

Two Argentinean soldiers were now stood in front of James and myself. I fired four or five times and a man was down. But James was completely frozen on the floor. The Argentinean soldier still standing took advantage of this, was standing firing away at James. In the pool of blood he was sitting in, I knew he was dead. I could sense my eyes filling up, but I was going to fall. I had to get myself out of here alive as the Argentinean was now aiming his gun at me. He stopped to reload and I quickly reloaded my gun as well. I fired at the soldier many times until he was down and gone.

I'd never be able to forgive myself for killing someone and taking a life, but this time it was different. He killed *my* good friend, and it hurts inside to watch and not be able to do anything to stop the innocent man's life being taken away in a matter of seconds.

He deserved what was coming to him.

Harriet Grainger (14)
Whitburn CE School, Whitburn

A Day In The Life Of A Dragon Slayer

Do you know how hard it is being a dragon slayer? Well firstly they're absolutely humungous and if that's not enough they fly and breathe fire! As well as that they continue fighting until you completely butcher their every limb or pierce their very heart. It's hard, life. You have to risk everything, not that I have much but anyhow, and then you get no recognition; last time I only got a few potatoes. If the king still thinks I'll slay every dragon in his kingdom for that measly prize he can think again.

There are good sides, I mean, I have travelled the country, met lots of friendly but weird folk who make slaying much more interesting and you get the best fresh dragon meat to eat and sell, did I tell you it's delicious? However my favourite part is saving the damsel in distress, some are so beautiful, but none really want a long-term relationship with a person who could die next week. So I'm still on the lookout for Miss Right.

Well there are ups and downs I suppose, but last week was nearly my last. It was Goth the Great's turn for the chop; she's the most ferocious and biggest dragon in the whole of the West Country but not the biggest I've killed, but that's another story. I thought she was dead, a definite gonner.

As I walked away in triumph she sprang upon me and began to crush me under her foot, oh the pain as her foot-long, diamond-sharp claws pierced my armour with ease and slowly reached my skin . . .

'Oi peasant boy, stop daydreaming, how much are your apples?' came a customer's voice from over the stall.

Josh Welsh (14)
Whitburn CE School, Whitburn

A Day In The Life Of A Pickled Onion

I was awoken by the light of the refrigerator, this is unusual as I have just been shipped in from Belgium on the cargo ship. I was in a huge box, it was dark but the luminous vinegar showed me where to move. Sitting in the jar was really uncomfortable as all of the other pickled onions were squashing me into the corner. Oh no! It was a circular jar. How can they squash me into the corner?

As the day progressed Mrs Jenkins was unloading the shopping into the refrigerator, I waited anxiously as she knocked and bashed the jar, my skin was beginning to fall off. I felt as though I was a failure as a pickled onion. Then suddenly Mrs Jenkins' son Jamal appeared and reached for the pickled onion jar, he had it in his hand and tried to twist the jar open and suddenly he fractured his wrist. I thought to myself that I would never get eaten. The refrigerator door closed and I sat wondering what to do. Then I had a crazy thought; I'd kill myself, but then forgot I couldn't get out of the jar, oh fiddlesticks!

So I sat, but nothing happened . . . but suddenly Janie, Mr and Mrs Jenkins' daughter came and she opened the jar and she put me on a plate. She then took me through to the dining room. Instead of eating me straight away she threw me up high into the atmosphere, *woooo* and then I plummeted down like a cannonball from a cannon, she missed and I rolled onto the floor. I was now of no use. She put me straight into the dark, dirty rubbish-filled bin! *Nooo!*

Sam Harwood (13)
Whitburn CE School, Whitburn

A Day In The Life Of William Shakespeare

(Based on William Shakespeare and the theatre)

'Morning Willy!' shouted Percy, in his hard Irish accent.

'Morning Mr P!' He took a breath and looked at Mr P. 'How's you, you dirty, frostbitten, rabbit muncher?'

'Good, good, long day ahead of us today laddy, we have to perform two plays as the Queen is coming to give us a rating,' moaned Percy, while shuffling the props around on the stage.

'Better get to work then!' yelled William over the hall as he tried his clothes on.

The chime rang and The Globe filled up extremely quickly with many different people, all of the spectators were selling, buying and throwing rotten fruit around, apples, pears, tomatoes and bananas, all mashed up on the stage.

'I don't like this Percy!' whispered William, leaning over Percy's shoulder.

'I don't either but we have to do it, think positive.'

Splat! A green and red, maggot-infested tomato skimmed past William's face.

'Urgh!' he screamed.

'Cut this piece of filth off me!' he kept on screaming.

By this time, lots of the crowd were trying to make him more nervous and pull him off the stage.

'I've got to do this Percy!'

'You will William!'

The crowd went quiet for a few seconds and then William started to act at the play.

A few hours later and the play had finished, all of the spectators had exited the building. William and Percy went behind stage to clean their clothes of rotten fruit.

'It wasn't that bad now was it William?'

'No, definitely not, thou shall not panic any more,' shouted William, while cleaning the banana out of his eyes.

Jonathon McCulley (13)
Whitburn CE School, Whitburn

A Day In The Life Of William Shakespeare
(Based on William Shakespeare and his theatre)

'We need to be ready for our next performance.' I was telling the actors that they had to be ready for Henry VIII. I get really angry with the actors at times. While the plays go on, I'd write my next play and be King John. I was writing history. This was my second to last category to write. My next and last category, would be poetry. Comedy was my first category and the category I have just completed was tragedy. People would be coming in soon and we were about 4-5 minutes behind time.

'Thou perished, dog-eared dogfish,' I called an actor this because he was getting on my nerves. The groundlings were starting to drift into the theatre, I stood at the door for a couple of minutes and then I went back to my office. Now almost everyone was in. In about 2-3 minutes, the performance would begin. Here it was, the music played and the actors came out.

After about half an hour, one of the actors made a mistake in speech and some of the groundlings threw rotten fruit at him. This annoyed me greatly. That only happened once fortunately. Then it was the end of the show. The groundlings and the actors left and the cleaners cleaned up the rotten fruit. That was another performance over. The theatre was then locked.

Next week I will be writing King John and I can't wait. I am also excited writing poetry.

Stephen Pollard (13)
Whitburn CE School, Whitburn

A Day In The Life Of Matt Dawson

It's the World Cup Final. Ten seconds to go in extra time. The score is 17-17. I knew if I made a bit more ground, a kick would be in Jonny Wilkinsons' range. I heard our captain Martin Johnson asking the referee how long was left. 'Two minutes,' he replied. A ruck was formed, the ball was ready to be passed to Jonny. However, I picked the ball up and ran through the Australian defence but I was tackled by Wendle Sailor on the 22-metre line. Our forwards came flying over the top of me. Martin Johnson picked up the ball and made more ground so I could make the final pass to Jonny, so he could kick the magical drop goal to bring us World Cup glory. I passed the ball and boom, he drop kicked it. Through the posts it went. The crowd went wild. I was so excited all I could shout was, 'World Cup!'

I asked the ref how long was left, he said, 'Time is up when the ball next goes out of play.' I told Martin Johnson to tell whoever get the ball from the restart to kick the ball out of play. Up it went, out of Elton Flatley's hands and off his boot into the air. I saw Neil Black catch the ball and pass it to Mike Catt who booted it into touch.

The final whistle went. We were the new World Champions.

As the trophy was brought out, the Australian team congratulated us and then received their runners-up medals. After that I led the team onto the stand to receive our medals. Martin Johnson came out last to receive the glamorous Golden Webb Ellis Trophy and to lift it high into the air to symbolise it was coming back to its home country.

Five hours passed and we were in the bar. I was planning to get really drunk as it was a day of celebration. However, a bad announcement was made, George Gregan, Martin Johnson and Neil Back announced they were retiring from international rugby.

However today turned out to be a really good day and maybe the best day of my life.

Michael Booth (13)
Whitburn CE School, Whitburn

A Day In The Life Of An Apple

Today I was in pain, just sitting in the fruit bowl, Bob went to pick me up to eat me, then he looked at all of them. Those painful bruises because when his stupid mother was taking me home in the shopping bag, she dropped the bag and all of the heavy stuff fell on me. It really hurt me.

Again, it happened to me, but it was Bob's stupid little sister Sarah. She picked me up, looked at all of the bruises but this was different, she saw them and then in shock, she threw me up. I landed on the hard floor. She didn't even try to pick me up because their pet dog, Ginger, started biting me and playing with me as if I was its ball. Back and forward I went for hours, until she got really tired and went to lie down.

After hours of just lying on the floor, I had split skin, the doors of my juicy inside were open, like the dog had just let a load of dust get into my house.

It became night. Still, I was just lying on the floor, helplessly, like a person stranded on a rock, in the middle of the sea.

The next morning a spider came down from the window sill. I just lay there helplessly, and that spider had its big, red eyes set on me. It came towards me and didn't look like it was going to slow down, let alone stop. I was scared out of my skin.

Seconds later, Mrs Doohicky came flying down from the sky. Although apples don't have legs, she did. She jumped down out of the fruit bowl and off the ledge. She put her own life on the line to save mine, and luckily, that super woman apple came down and nailed that evil spider right in-between the eyes.

I felt so happy because Mrs Doohicky came down to save me, and then took me to the top of the ledge, and took me back to the fruit bowl.

Many, many days later, I went all mouldy so Bob's mam, Sue threw me in the bin . . .

Jonathon Phinn (12)
Whitburn CE School, Whitburn

The Creature

One cold, dark evening I was sitting down having my dinner when I heard a strange sound. I looked out of my window to see a strange creature. Its arms and hands were like knives ready to slice through my neck. It had no mouth but three slots instead and spoke telepathically. It had the body of a centaur which must have made the thing 7ft tall as it stared at me. Its snake-like eyes fixed in the head of a bull. I reached for my gun but it wasn't there. When I looked outside again, it was there, sitting in the palm of one of his six hands, two of which were human. Then, with one slash of his knife-like hand my shotgun was in two.

I went to ring the police but instead I rang the National Guard. They were at my door within minutes of me calling. They knocked loudly on my door and asked me what the problem was. I told them about 'the creature' and they asked to see it. I quickly took them to the window where I'd seen 'the creature' but it had gone. Vanished. We had a large argument about 'the creature' but in the end they left and fined me £100 for wasting their time. They said that I was crazy, but I know that I saw 'the creature'.

James Seward (12)
Whitburn CE School, Whitburn

The Truth

A long time ago, about 1332 there was a monastery that was always locked. It was on high ground and it had big broad iron gates that were painted black with big points on them. People say that there are evil things that happen but nobody really knows the truth. People say they have seen monks in the building and they are very right.

A young man went into the monastery but never returned. He knocked on the door and was dragged in by a monk. Inside there was screaming and people who'd been hung and they looked like they had been there for a 100 years. He saw people burnt and their carcasses piled on top of each other. He saw a man tarred and feathered with his legs chopped off. It was living hell.

A monk took him to a table and strapped him down. The monk picked up a pen and gouged out his left eye. People have asked me how I know this and the truth is I am that young man.

Morgan Lowrie (12)
Whitburn CE School, Whitburn

A Day In The Life Of Mojo Harrison (My Dog)

This morning, I lay in bed until about 10.30, then I got up and went downstairs, I ate my breakfast of scrambled eggs and ham, then went outside to do my business. When I came back inside, I finished off my dad's cup of tea. After that I went back to bed until midday, when I came downstairs my dad put my harness on me and took me for my afternoon walk.

He took me to the beach and threw sticks in the sea for me to chase, when I went in the sea I had a little swim, then we walked along to Morrisons, my dad went inside and bought a bottle of water, he took a drink then poured some in his hand for me to drink then we walked back home through the park.

We got home, I went to bed until my sister got home from school at 3.45, she got changed and did her homework, then took me to the new fields with her friends, we came back home for about 8.30pm, I went to bed at 9.30pm, chewed a bone for about half an hour, then drifted off to sleep.

Megan Harrison (12)
Whitburn CE School, Whitburn

My Adventure With Medusa

It was a cold, blustery day, yet the sun was shining brightly. As I walked down the street, a man came running up to me, his hat blowing off his head as he ran.

'Katie, Katie, Medusa has struck again,' he yelled as if he thought I could do anything about her. You see Medusa had powers, she could turn people into stone with one glance. Many heroes had been lost in the world of stone.

I went down to the lake to watch the sun go down and I suddenly realised it was time. I climbed onto Pegasus (my flying horse) and went to Medusa's lair. If it wasn't such an emergency then I would have taken the long route, past the sun and through the clouds.

Medusa's lair was dark and cold, with spiders climbing up the walls of the cave. Not the tiniest streak of sun got into the darkness. As I walked into the lair, a tremendous stench met my nose. It was a damp smell, a worrying smell, a smell that would put you off going in.

I tiptoed in and the lair was so quiet, you could have heard a mouse scuttle across the damp floor, or a pin being dropped. There was a mysterious look about the lair, like a murder case waiting to be solved. I turned around with horror, as a cackling laughter met my ears. There she was, the woman that had a beautiful face with snakes for hair. Then I noticed her eyes . . .

Kathryn Gill (12)
Whitburn CE School, Whitburn

A Day In The Life Of A World War II Child

As I walked down the brown old staircase, I could hear my mother talking to my older brother Tom about a recent raid.

'You know Mrs Goodman from Maiden Way? Well her house got bombed last night, she is in a right state,' Mother said, sounding worried.

'Where is she staying?' I said, picking up a plate of breakfast which was nothing special.

'She is staying in the church hall with every other victim of the raid,' said Mother sighing.

Mother's eyes caught a glimpse of a photograph of Father and sighed again, she missed him dearly ever since he went away to sea to fight. We are all very proud of him but miss him a lot, he has been gone for months, it seems like years. Tom sat quietly, he misses Father the most, he has been very depressed lately.

'Will you be a dear Catherine, will you do down to the corner shop to pick up our daily rations? The ration book is on the desk, maybe Mr Hunter has a treat for us?' asked Mother.

There was a knock at the door, a man wearing a navy blue uniform with a cap. 'Telegram for Mrs Brown,' he said. Mother came rushing to the door, she ripped the carefully sealed envelope and the telegram read:

'Dear my darling wife,

This only short but I am just letting you know that I am healthy and well. Hope to see you soon,

Richard

PS Hope you children are being good for your mother'.

Victoria Heselton (12)
Whitburn CE School, Whitburn

Lost Lovers

It was October, just a few days before Hallowe'en. A mist lay over the country road that Sarah and Paul were driving along. Suddenly Sarah caught the scent of something burning. Paul stopped to check the car. He lifted the bonnet to find the radiator was steaming. Sarah stepped out of the car to get some fresh air. Spotting an old rotten oak tree with flowers laid at the roots, she walked over to read the note beside them. It read: 'To my darling one, I will love you always and I will never forget you, Pete'.

'Paul,' Sarah whispered, 'I think someone died here.'

Sarah walked to the car to get her phone to ring breakdown services. As she turned, two figures appeared out of the mist, walking towards them. The man offered Paul some help while Sarah chatted to the woman.

'The car's fixed, do you want a life home?' Paul asked them.

Sarah asked the couple what they had been doing in the middle of nowhere, the man replied that his wife had died there a few months ago, after a car accident.

A silence fell upon them. Paul stopped the car, only the man stepped out thanking Sarah and Paul. Confused, Sarah asked Paul where the woman was and Paul, looking puzzled, asked her what she was talking about.

Sarah realised who the woman really was.

Jenny Johnston (11)
Whitburn CE School, Whitburn

A Day In The Life Of A Hockey Player

One morning I woke up raring to go, we had a hockey game against Coventry Blaze, it was going to be a tough one but we were ready to play.

We were playing at the Newcastle Metro Arena. When we arrived and they arrived, we started to get ready to play. My friend was just about ready when he put on his elbow pad and it snapped, he panicked but luckily I had a spare, which I said he could borrow. We were ready to play, the ice was ready, we lined up to go on and we entered the ice, the crowd was roaring, the music was playing, we did our warm-up, then went to the net for a chant.

We shouted: *'1, 2, 3, Sunderland,'* and the referee blew the whistle for the face off. We went to our positions.

He dropped the puck, the game had begun. It was a tough first period, but we scraped a lead, the buzzer went, end of first period. They cut the ice and sent us on for the second period.

Oh no they scored, we were going to have to fight now, wait, he shot and he scored - what a goal. That period went extremely fast and then it was the third and final period. The last period, it was anyone's game.

I carried the puck past the blue line. Shot - *Yes!* Bottom right, what a goal and suddenly the hooter went. It was over, we shook hands and lined up for Man of the Match. It went to number 39 - Calum Ross. We went to get changed and celebrated.

Calum Ross (12)
Whitburn CE School, Whitburn

Hercules' Story

One day Hercules, the son of Zeus, was assigned a mission to defeat Medusa, the three-headed snake. Hercules was warned that if you chopped off one of the heads, another two heads grew back.

A few days later Hercules was sent off on the mission and he was travelling for three days and three nights to The Valley of the Dead to face Medusa. At about midday Hercules arrived at where he was supposed to meet Medusa. He was waiting in The Valley of the Dead for an hour or two, and she was all purple and a huge monstrous beast with three heads.

Hercules had forgotten what his father had told him about Medusa so then straight away Medusa went for the kill at Hercules and he chopped her head off and saw that she'd grown back another two heads. All of a sudden Hercules remembered what his father had told him.

So then Hercules pulled out his sword and lit it with fire and threw it straight into the eye and its eye on fire and blinded it. He then fired the arrow into its heart and Medusa was defeated. Hercules was the winner.

Neil Atkinson (12)
Whitburn CE School, Whitburn

The Earth And The Moon

A cat, dog, mouse and cheese are like a food chain, mouse eats cheese, cat eats mouse and dog chases cat but in the following food chain, there are two things in it and these things are why the Earth spins.

It all started when a little planet called the moon shouted to a planet called Earth. 'Hey! Earth you stinky, horrible planet! Give me a sweet!'

'What was that? Come here you!' And so the moon started running round the Earth. The Earth couldn't run because his shoes were too big, so instead he twirled around and around snarling at the moon and he hasn't stopped yet!

So that's why the Earth spins because he's chasing that cheeky little planet called the moon.

Daniel Patterson (12)
Whitburn CE School, Whitburn

A Day In The Life Of A Victorian Child

Hello, my name is Kate and I am 8 years old. I go to a school called Buxton Primary School and I am in Year 4.

My teacher is called Mr Green and is very nice but can sometimes be strict when you are naughty.

My day starts with me getting up and dressed. It doesn't take me very long to get washed, dressed and to have my breakfast. Then I start my journey to school. I have to walk along two streets and across the village park which takes me about half an hour.

Once I get to school I meet all my friends and we talk until the bell goes. Then when we get inside we have to be silent while Mr Green takes the register, I come 4th in the register because my second name is Cuthbertson.

The 1st lesson we have is maths and we are learning our times table but I'm really bad at them and I don't like the teacher - Mrs Burton because she thinks I'm not answering the questions on purpose.

Uh oh! Mrs Burton is coming over to me while I'm writing about my life.

'Kate, what are you doing?' Mrs Burton says.

'I'm . . . I'm . . . w-r-i-t-i-n-g a-b-o-u-t . . . '

'Oh Kate get on with it,' shouts Mrs Burton.

'I'm writing about my life story,' I say.

'That is not acceptable,' Mrs Burton says. *'Right, that deserves six of the best, come here child!'*

Jessica Machin (12)
Whitburn CE School, Whitburn

A Day In The Life Of William Shakespeare

(Based on William Shakespeare and the theatre)

'One actor has broken his leg,' exclaimed Percy.

'Thou shall not panic as I can replace the actor as Henry the VIII,' I exclaimed.

As I walked on stage I heard loud cheers, hissing and booing, but I thought to myself, *the show must go on.*

We began, everything was well until a groundling took to his feet and began to scream, *'Fire! Fire!'*

All of the audience fled, crushing into one another to exit through the door. As I stood there not knowing what to do, Percy came up to me. 'We better get going or we'll be burnt alive.'

I agreed. I began to make my way passed the helpless bodies lying on the floor.

We eventually made our way to the grey cobbled streets looking shocked. Percy entered my line of vision and tried to make me go back. I refused and ran home as fast as I could.

Later that night I sat awake all night thinking what would happen to the theatre.

Early morning a messenger came round telling me a new theatre would be built called 'The Globe Theatre'. I was so happy and so excited I ran round the streets singing with glee.

It took many years to build The Globe but when it was finished it was a masterpiece and it held many more audiences and less groundlings than before. I made one speech in The Globe which was, 'You're mine until death do us part'.

Gary Moon (13)
Whitburn CE School, Whitburn

A Day In The Life Of William Shakespeare

(Based on William Shakespeare and the theatre)

'Get up, you'll all be late for work!' bellowed Mrs Shakespeare as she rolled her husband off the bed, onto the cold, hard floor.

'Why did you do that?' grunted William.

Ten minutes later William Shakespeare was dashing out the front door onto the streets of London, on his way to The Globe.

He arrived just as the first groundlings were entering The Globe. As he stumbled around the back he met the actors getting changed for the play which happened to be Henry V.

'Good morning all,' he shouted because the groundlings were shouting in the pit.

'Come on men we'll be late,' shouted William.

William went to his seat to watch the play; he always did.

'Henry, we shall go to war!' the actors were saying.

Everything was going well until a statue of Henry with a flame attached was lowered, the ropes slipped, the flames dropped, the stage set alight almost immediately.

'Fire! Fire!' yelled the groundlings. The Globe Theatre burned for two hours . . .

Shakespeare sat on the sidewalk looking at the ashes of his life's work, as he sat with his hands on his face he realised that he had lost more than The Globe, he had lost many of his closest friends. He had lost everything . . .

Mark Lindsley (13)
Whitburn CE School, Whitburn

A Day In The Life Of Macbeth

Macbeth shall sleep no more. Never again shall I know the rapture of a tranquil slumber. The tales told of my conscience shatter my repose like so much glass; stories of my own guilt fog my mind.

How I wish I had not the simple capacity to feel. Oh, to possess the same numbness as my hard-hearted queen. My guilt is a weakening force. I hath slain the gracious Duncan for my own fruitless crown, the crown which the weird women promised. However, the thought of Banquo and what he knows crawls through my mind like a scorpion, every word of his penetrating me. Like any worthy friend he would watch over me, but I fear he does so too closely. This is a conundrum, however, that will soon be remedied. I hath marched *noble* Banquo to meet his fearful demise. Two sinful men have been sent to do this deed, I convinced them to do it; challenged their masculinity and twisted their thoughts to make them believe what I wanted them to. So, on this very night Banquo shall ride with Fleance, not expecting what shall be bestowed unto him and his precious offspring. The righteous blood of Banquo shall soon be nothing but a mere stain on a cutthroat's hand.

Emma Jayne Nagouse (13)
Whitburn CE School, Whitburn

Night Life

As we pull up to Jess' house and got out of the car, I felt a hand on my shoulder. I jumped around startled. 'Jack!' I felt myself go crimson, my cheeks burning. (Not only is Jack Jessie's friend, but he is mega cute and all the girls love him.) '

'Hi Emily.'

'Hi,' I stuttered, still a little surprised.

'Are you here to go camping with Jess?'

'Yeah! Are you going too?' I said hopefully.

'Yes!'

Great! Jess invited Jack, it will be more fun that way.

When Jess invited me to her camping birthday party, I knew it would be a laugh, just me and her in the American wilderness, even though I'm not an outdoorsy person, but she promised we wouldn't have to go camping, just help pitch the tent, eat our picnic and enjoy the scenery. It sounded OK.

As we sat in the back of Jessie's dad's van and gave Jessie her presents, we sang silly songs, giggled about stupid jokes and constantly moaned, 'Are we there yet?'

Eventually, after a long, bumpy ride, we reached Camp Rosewood and set off on yet another long journey to decide where to pitch the tent. Jack said we didn't need a map. Big mistake!

After wandering for what seemed like hours, we decided we were lost. But Jessie always looks on the bright side. 'Why don't we camp here? It's nice.'

So we did.

Soon it began to get dark and we settled down inside the tent. After all our hard work and, having eaten our food, we were very tired and soon fell asleep. But at about eleven o'clock we were all woken suddenly by an inhuman, gasping scream. In the dim light of the moon we stared at each other horrified. It seemed closer, more horrific the second time we heard it. Jack eased the zip on the tent opening. We stared, transfixed, at the floating bright lights bobbing in the trees . . .

Eve Calvert (11)
Whitburn CE School, Whitburn

A Day In The Life Of A Bird

Ouch that hurt! Oh it's them silly children again. I don't know how they find pleasure in throwing stones at my nest. One day I'll go down there and give them a piece of my mind. Well, I'll let my beak do all the work.

I woke up yesterday to the sound of the cockerel, Benny. He lives at the farm just down the road. My eyes were suddenly flooded with light, I quickly closed them again. Eventually I woke up properly and looked out over the park. Fresh dewdrops were still soaking up the first sunlight, they glinted all colours - green, purple and pink. There was a slight breeze. The grass danced, still drinking up the moist dew. My tree was in full bloom with great green leaves stretching out, worshipping the sun. Bright yellow lemons, plump and juicy, hung from the tree. I opened my wings and glided across the park to the street opposite. I sat on one of the roofs and sang a sweet song, chirping happily while people walked passed, stopping and listening with content at my tune.

I then flew to the house on the corner and took an early morning bath while waiting for the people who owned the house to give me my breakfast of chopped up bread, oats and occasionally rice. My sister suddenly landed next to me, so we did a little greeting dance. We ate our breakfast together and she flew home, so did I. I landed just short of the branch and fell to the ground. I was in such pain, I couldn't stand up. I realised I was in the middle of a road; I wasn't at home at all. Suddenly a giant green monster roared passed me. It nearly ran me over. I could smell the fumes coming from it, it made me feel sick.

Some time after, five large pink things picked me up and held me softly. 'It's OK little birdie, I've got you.' I was too weak to see what it was; before I knew it I was asleep.

When I woke up I was in some sort of metal house with bright shiny bars. I was in a cage. A little girl was stroking me. I couldn't find the strength to peck her, I was actually enjoying it.

The family nursed me back to health so now I live with them, well, some of the time. They let me come and go as I please and I like it that way. So that is a day in the life of a bird and I hope it lasts for many days to come.

Rachael Buckley (11)
Whitburn CE School, Whitburn

The Attic

Outside my bedroom door at the top of the stairs is the attic hatch. I was in the house alone and began to think about the attic.

The wind was howling loudly outside. The phone rang and I went downstairs, glancing up at the hatch which was closed. Mam was on the phone to say she would be late. I wondered if I should go to my gran's or not.

As I went back up the stairs, I looked at the hatch and was sure I saw it move. I shook my head, telling myself not to be daft. Sitting at my desk I forgot about the hatch.

Afterwards I went into the bathroom, I couldn't resist a glance at the hatch. It was closed. When I came out I heard a quiet thud and looked up to see the hatch close.

I decided to go to my gran's after all. I told her about the hatch. She laughed and said there was no such thing as ghosts. I hadn't mentioned ghosts and began to wonder.

Mam collected me. I asked about the attic and she also laughed, saying there was nothing up there but junk, and definitely no ghosts.

At home again I climbed the stairs. The hatch dropped shut just as Mam closed the front door.

'There, look!' I shouted.

Mam laughed saying, 'Don't be silly, it's just the draught from opening the door.' That made sense, so I forgot about the hatch and the attic.

As I lay in bed, the house was still and the doors were closed. Then I heard the thud from above!

Who knows what is in the attic!

Alex Rea (11)
Whitburn CE School, Whitburn

A Day In The Life Of Macbeth

Dear Diary,

Today has been memorable. After a long and bloody battle with the rebel swines, it is clear that desertion is not an advisable practise to follow, this made evident by the victory of King Duncan's army over the rebel scum's meagre force.

There have been other events besides the battle that showed themselves to be just as memorable. Banquo, a good friend and superb warrior, though in my eyes he does seem a tad bit unimaginative, has been my companion for many years. We have both fought together and left together, and while proceeding along the heath towards camp we encountered what seemed to be three witches. It would be true to say that they were women but their beards forced me to believe otherwise. These strange beings entrusted me with information that was as surprising as it was dangerous. Not only did they know that I was Thane of Glamis, they hailed me Thane of Cawdor and King hereafter. I listened to their strange words with fascination. Banquo, of course, was his usual self; nodding quietly, looking sceptical and completely unaffected by his prophecy of a line of kings. It would seem fate has smiled on me.

Anthony Johnson (14)
Whitburn CE School, Whitburn

A Day In The Life Of Banquo

This morning was fine until I remembered that today was Macbeth's coronation and that I must attend, oh how I resent this day. Macbeth, he has it all now - King, Cawdor and Glamis. I believe there is something foul going on, it has been since we met those hideous hags upon the heath. I believe they have plagued his mind with the thoughts of king. I, on the other hand, have managed to put the predictions that were proclaimed to me at the back of my mind as I have more important matters to contend with.

Later in the day he came out with this remark of how I am his chief guest. He knows that I am nothing but a thorn in his side and that I should be done away with; must now fear for my life as what I think may come true, Macbeth has the power to do as he pleases. Again, before I go for my ride, Macbeth comes out with another of his pointless remarks, which he hopes will entrap me in his little plot to kill me. He whispered in my ear, 'I hear our bloody cousins are bestowed in England and in Ireland, not confessing their cruel parricide.' But this does affect me I know that Macbeth killed Duncan all along and that Macbeth keeps lying to make sure nobody catches onto him. Sooner or later he shall be caught out. I shall now go out for a ride.

Matthew Hage (14)
Whitburn CE School, Whitburn

A Day In The Life Of Banquo

(From William Shakespeare's Macbeth)

Dear Diary,

I woke up this grey and dull morning to remember that it was the day of deceitful Macbeth's coronation, and so this meant I was to attend. However, I did not want to watch such a coronation because Macbeth now has all of the glory. He has now become king; Cawdor, Glamis, all.

After returning from the cruel coronation of King Macbeth, which was unnecessary because of the death of King Duncan, I thought he may well have become king by foul means and unfair play. The two-faced liar asked me to attend his supper, even though I knew what he was trying to do. He thought I did not know that he was up to something. Consequently I told him that I was going to ride with my son Fleance, which made him very angry, I could see it in his face.

He has been telling many lies to me and he was running out of cunning ideas - he did not have many in the first place. I fear very strongly that moaning Macbeth had something to do with the death of Duncan.

Me and my beloved son, Fleance, are going riding tonight and may try and attend the feast. I am not sure if I should go to the supper as Macbeth may have something planned.

Craig Young (14)
Whitburn CE School, Whitburn

Diary Of Macbeth

The blanket of darkness had been cast upon us like a fisherman casting his wondrous net. The stench of rotten corpses and fresh blood stabbed me in the back. We were victorious; the blood spilled could have made a massacred ocean. Myself, and worthy Banquo, were barely wounded, only tattered and tired.

An eerie, unearthly silence echoed throughout the valley; it was deserted and all that could be seen were ghastly shadows. A silent cursing murmur sailed through the air making my hair stand on end. Three hideous figures formed a circle as we passed a dismal boulder. They called themselves Women, yet their beards forbade me to interpret that they were. I feared them confusingly and Banquo remained with no comments.

They came with spectacular news; I will soon be Thane of Cawdor and King hereafter. At first I didn't believe these tools of dark wisdom but I was later informed that I was dressed in the worthy thane's robe - had we eaten from the insane root to see all of this?

Upon the blasted heath they stopped our way, with such prophetic greeting. I charged them to speak but they vanished. I needed to gain more knowledge if I was to become a king.

So many of today's feelings sink deeply in my conscience; the rain of blood, amount of inevitable death and these monstrous creatures. I feel excited and ambitious. I am also very confused. All of this pressure is driving me to the edge. I can't tell if I am alive and dreaming, or dead and remembering.

Louie Crake (14)
Whitburn CE School, Whitburn

A Day In The Life Of Groundling George
(Based on William Shakespeare's theatre)

The plum was resting in my hand. Hamlet had just commenced. Rain lashed at my dirty face as I watched the peevish play. 'I did not pay a penny for this rank drama.' I held the plum and aimed.

Some superior to me bellowed, 'Thou waggish clay-brained dogfish!' and hurled a rotten apple at my face. He approached madly with fiery anger flickering in his eyes. 'Thou dare insult that work of art! You should be taken away and hung!' He pulled me nearer to his clean, rich clothes. 'You vacant groundling, you're not worth a penny, you don't come close.'

He pushed me towards the muck of the ground, smothering it foully in my face. I know that I should have walked away, but no, I did not, I pushed the plum in his face and clenched my muddy first, ready.

He threw me a smile as he called out for the men to arrest me. They grabbed my arms, pulling me away. I did not struggle. I knew I was beaten.

'Can I ask one thing my man?'

'Go ahead groundling,' the gentleman with my arms uttered.

'Who was that man?' I questioned.

'You mean you do not know?' he chuckled.

'Why it's the only playwright Sir William Shakespeare.'

I suddenly felt like a real greasy clay-brained pantaloon. I had just quarrelled with Shakespeare. And to add salt to injury, had badly named his play.

I was laughing at as I was carted away. 'Thou piggish dogfish! one laughed.

At this moment I thought, *thou play was not bad!*

Nikita Young (13)
Whitburn CE School, Whitburn

A Day In The Life Of An Actor

(Based upon William Shakespeare and the theatre)

Leo woke up at 8am feeling terrified. He hardly slept a wink last night, he was too nervous. 'It's the big play tonight,' he said to himself. Leo was nervous because everybody was going to be watching, including the Queen.

Leo went to the round theatre where he worked and got his words and started to rehearse. His best friend, Stuart, was watching, acting as the audience, and there was one thing that Leo said that made him laugh. Leo stood there staring.

'That bit was not meant to be funny!'

'Sorry my dear friend, it was just the way you said it. It was hilarious,' chuckled Stuart.

'Well if you don't mind Stuart I'm trying to rehearse and I'm really nervous. If I don't do very well I shall be sacked.'

'Sorry Leo, I forgot this night is so important to you.'

'It doesn't matter anyway. Have you got any old clothes I can use as my costume?' questioned Leo.

'Yeah, I'll just go and get them for you.'

Later on at 7pm Leo walked up and down backstage.

'Stuart, I don't think I can do this.'

'Yes you can, don't be stupid, you'll be fine.'

'Mr Shakespeare won't be happy if I mess up my words.'

'Well just do your best, now go.'

After the show . . .

'Well done you've done it, you're the star of the show.'

'I know, I can't believe it, it must have been what I said, thou greasy clay-brained conker blossom.'

'Yeah and I wonder how you'll do next time.'

Zoe Ross (13)
Whitburn CE School, Whitburn

A Day As Banquo

'Our blood hath spilt in valour on the battlefield.'

'Here, here Macbeth, why hath you not rejoiced at the famous victory at war?' I asked.

'I felt it not necessary,' replied Macbeth. 'Yes we won a great and noble victory but my disgust in the traitor, Thane of Cawdor, sticks deep, we should not celebrate under this disloyal scum!'

'Was it really true that he betrayed us?' I wondered.

'Yes indeed my great friend, he found sides with MacDonwald,' sighed Macbeth.

I stood on the spot remembering all the people I had killed during the battle and wished I had set my anger on that of Thane of Cawdor.

'Banquo,' asked Macbeth, 'why linger when we should be moving? The king awaits us!'

Myself and Macbeth travelled far that day as far as to the heath. At that moment we were approached by withered hags or so what looked like hags but their beards forbade me to interpret them.

'What are these things?' I whispered.

'I don't know but keep quiet do not force them to speak,' replied Macbeth.

We both kept quiet but they spoke first in a low raspy whisper.

'All hail Macbeth, hail to thee, Thane of Glamis, Thane of Cawdor, that shalt be king hereafter,' they chanted.

Macbeth looked astonished and gaped open mouthed at the witches. He managed to say a few words. 'I . . . I know I am Thane of Glamis, but Cawdor and king, what is this all about?'

'Ahh yes, your fortunes are to become high and great but do not fear power for you shall be king,' they cried.

Daniel Parnaby (13)
Whitburn CE School, Whitburn

A Day In The Life Of Macbeth

(In Acts 1, Scene 3)

The sky was as red as blood as Banquo and I walked along. We were talking about the day's events in battle, about the lives lost on both sides, when out of nowhere there shone three shiny witches in the middle of the road.

Banquo portrayed the foul beasts to a great extent, he described their physical features in a way that sent shivers down your spine, he left no detail out.

Understandably I could not believe my ears as the next part of this encounter was shocking, shocking enough that if I was not thinking about how to achieve what the witches had spoken, I very well may have died. Out of the blue the hags hailed me as Thane of Glamis, Thane of Cawdor and king hereafter. How could this be, I pondered quietly to myself, the Thane of Cawdor lives and so does the graceful King Duncan.

Again a weird thing happened. Moments after hailing me king, they hailed Banquo the father in a line of kings. Odd how the creatures would hail me king and then change their prediction to suit Banquo. I knew that if the Devil does speak true, I would have to get rid of Banquo sooner than later.

Straightaway the prophecies were becoming true as Ross and Angus appeared and said that I was to become Thane of Cawdor. At first I could not believe what I was hearing. I was thinking, *why do they dress me in borrowed robe?*

Matthew Porter (14)
Whitburn CE School, Whitburn

A Day In The Life Of Macbeth

On this day, blood had been spilt upon the horizon.

The battle had been fought valiantly and viciously; lots of men had lost friends, family and even their own lives. They fought for their king and country, but only one army prevailed. Us. The battle was long and hard but we were not only fighting for our king, but for our own lives too, even though many had been lost. The opposition slashing at you with all of their might, the blows either shattering your bones or striking with your sword or shield. You literally could hardly catch your breath because the battle was so intense!

After the battle movement was impossible without tripping over a body. When we met up with friends after the fighting had stopped, you could hardly speak without shouting.

On the way to report to Duncan, the victory drum started its rampage. Then out of the darkness three horrifying ghostly figures appeared. They started speaking to me and Banquo. They said some things to me that sounded good. They promised me Glamis, Cawdor and to be king. I trusted these mythical creatures but I don't think that Banquo did. This may have only been because they promised that only his children would be king. This worried me. Anyway when I questioned these creatures there was a sudden blast of smoke and they disappeared! So Banquo and I carried on to Duncan. Laughing and talking about the battle we had just won on the way, we were cheerful!

Callum Scrimgour (13)
Whitburn CE School, Whitburn

A Day In The Life Of Macbeth

Finally. 'I hast it now, King, Cawdor, Glamis, all!'

Though there has been but one entity rotting in my scorpion-infested mind, like a snake, taunting the bite, and this entity is Banquo.

'Thou shalt get kings?'

Ha! After tonight he shall not be so lucky. And the witches' final prophecy: corrupt it will be.

Banquo and as gracious as his son, will live no more. Invite them to my banquet I did, though I and the daggers of the dogs do not intend to see them. Tonight they ride . . . and fall! I can only hope that the skill of the murderers is as tuned as they claim, or maybe I might see Banquo again tonight.

My banquet tonight will be the final stage, to ensure my reign as king. If Banquo does not show his face, my line as king is secure!

The murderers I met for the second time this evening. They are the most ungodly beings. Characters similar to Satan in their evilness, if not they are his fear. I was forced to use my cunning in convincing them. I challenged their masculinity, comparing them to that of canines. Soon they shall unleash their true malevolent selves, as their minds, their simple minds, are set upon the just deed of killing treacherous Banquo. Though he has been my companion through many dangers, this is the path I must take.

Angus Monaghan (14)
Whitburn CE School, Whitburn

Harvey's Adventure

Hi! I'm Harvey. I'm a cat. I'll tell you what happened yesterday . . .

I had my breakfast then I went outside to play. I walked through the lush green grass. I went to the corner of the garden behind the little waterfall and climbed over the fence to Clover's house. She is my best friend. I squeezed under the gap in the gate into her garden. Luckily she was outside; she appeared to be chasing butterflies.

'Hi!' I called.

'I've been waiting for you!' she laughed.

She beckoned me over to the fence. We climbed over into the field. There we met Hugo; we don't get on with him well.

'Well, well, if it isn't the little squirts!' he teased.

'Leave us alone you big ginger bully!' I shouted. We walked away and we didn't see him again.

Soon after we played hide-and-seek in the long grass. Out of the corner of my eye I saw the horses being turned into the field. We continued playing but we got too close to the horses which must have scared them. There was a big stampede so me and Clover had to run back to the fence without being squashed. We just made it!

'I think I should go home now,' I said, breathing heavily.

We said goodbye and went home.

Jill Croft (12)
Whitburn CE School, Whitburn

The Legend Of The Friendly Werewolf

'Where is he?'

'Who?' the shopkeeper asked, looking confused.

'The werewolf named . . . Albert,' the hooded figure whispered.

'Oh Albert, he left 5 minutes ago. Who are you?'

'I'm Valhana the werewolf hunter.' And with that he disappeared.

Meanwhile a small flat had been rented and inside it was spotlessly clean but from the bed a tall brown creature that looked like a wolf started to sing, *'Oh what a beautiful morning, oh what a beautiful day!'* He looked in the mirror and said to himself, 'Hullo, Albert.' Then he got dressed, put on a hat and went out. He had fur as brown as the soil and large ears but despite this no one noticed him.

Eventually he came to a café and went inside. It had tiled walls and small oak doors. He asked a lady if he could buy a cake but, as she was about to serve him, Valhana burst in pointing at Albert and yelling, 'He is a werewolf!'

Everyone screamed and started running around while poor Albert was left shouting, 'Don't worry, I won't hurt you, I'm a vegetarian!'

But no one listened to him and the next thing he knew, Valhana had grabbed him and put him inside a truck.

Finally the truck stopped and Albert was thrown out into a dense mountain rainforest. Legend says that Albert the friendly werewolf still lives in that rainforest trying to hitch a ride back to the city.

Frances Richardson (12)
Whitburn CE School, Whitburn

Young Writers – That's Write! Write Up Your Street Vol I

167

The Legend Of Zorro II

Let me take you back 200 years to tell you the tale of Zorro. But this you wouldn't have heard before . . . this is Zorro II.

Elaina was Zorro's daughter and she was determined to kill Captain Gonzalez for killing some innocent slaves.

Elaina tacked up her horse, Hurricane, and fastened her black mask which had two eyeholes cut in it. She was out to finish Captain Gonzalez for killing three innocent slaves for her capture. She galloped out of her secret lair and along the empty, lonely streets of California, Spain.

She sneaked through the shadows leading Hurricane and tied him to the castle gate. Elaina thrashed her whip, twined it around the balcony and pulled herself up and jumped into the room, right above Captain Gonzales.

'You killed three innocent slaves so here are three cuts to remind you never to rule California again!' whispered Elaina and she cut a small 'Z' into Gonzalez's neck.

'Now to finish your reign over California for good Captain Gonzalez!' and Elaina slowly stabbed Captain Gonzalez and he slid to his painful death at a window overlooking the sunset over beautiful California.

Elaina ruled California for a long time, she was the best president they ever had, and her son reigned after her. Elaina's family generations ruled California for many years and were known as 'the family of Zorro'.

Anna Robinson (11)
Whitburn CE School, Whitburn

The Legend Of El Batty

'Twas a peaceful day in the valley of Pyry, the birds were singing, the sun was shining and El Batty was once again kidnapping the mayor.

'Help me,' shouted the mayor, 'don't just stand there, shoot it, it doesn't matter about me, just save yourselves.'

El Batty bit the mayor.

'OK, it doesn't matter about you, just save me, you incompetent fools!' screamed the mayor.

Then, moments later, *bang,* someone shot a shotgun and hit El Batty in the eye.

'Roar!' roared Batty dropping the mayor.

The mayor landed on a circus tent but he fell through and hit the ground with a thud.

The next day the mayor called in Bart Hunter, the man who specialised in bat hunting. Bart entered the mayor's office and said, 'Hello Mr Mayor. Right, where's the little pest so I can exterminate it?'

'Well Bart, it isn't really little and it lives on top of Stone Mountain.'

The mayor showed Bart a picture of El Batty. 'So do you think you can do it?' asked the mayor.

Later that day Bart set off for Stone Mountain. Higher and higher he climbed until finally he reached the top. When he was on his feet, he saw El Batty sleeping, so he quietly crept up and cut off its head. Blood spurted out and covered Bart from head to toe.

He collapsed in relief because he had saved the town from the mighty El Batty.

Michael Scott (12)
Whitburn CE School, Whitburn

Samson's Story

It was December of 1986, the snowiest month ever; no one was stirring not even a mouse, until . . .

'Cock-a-doodle-doo.' The cockerel rose and so the day began.

Lucy jumped out of bed as fast as lightning and got dressed. She pulled on her hat, gloves, scarf and wellies then ran down the stairs to her front garden. That's when it happened . . . Samson became part of the real world, and he enjoyed every moment of it!

Lucy made an enormous mound of light, white, gleaming, fluffy snow. Gradually she rolled it into a rather large ball, this became Samson's body. Next she rolled another ball and another ball and placed these on top of the first ball and Samson (snowman) started to look complete but not just yet. What would make Samson look real? What should his finishing touches be? Then she thought, *oh I know!* So she took off her hat and scarf and carefully placed them on the snowman, making sure he didn't fall. Next she stuck two long sticks in either side of the snowman making rather skinny arms. Then she placed on a bright orange carrot nose followed by pebble eyes, mouth and buttons, then lastly put her multicoloured gloves onto Samson's skinny twig-like arm. Samson actually looked real!

Lucy couldn't believe how magnificent he looked, she couldn't wait to show her parents, she was so excited. But when Lucy started to move, so did Samson. He was alive!

Jade Pape (11)
Whitburn CE School, Whitburn

King Cronos

It was sunrise in Treregorn. The lush green trees swayed in the cool calm of the day. In the capital city, Senria, King Cronos was walking in the grounds of Treenus, pondering. You see, he was at war with King Atihock, the evil king of Berethirn. King Cronos pondered for a whole hour before he went inside his glorious palace. Inside it was like you had just walked into an ice-cave. There were diamond statues everywhere, crystal chandeliers hung from the jewel-layered ceiling.

The next day he went out into the city centre and declared confidently, 'People of Senria, I come before you today to announce we will be sending a huge army to King Atihock's kingdom of Berethirn. I warn you all to expect a counter-attack!'

The crowd made it obvious they were worried as a murmur spread throughout the crowd. After the announcement the Treregorn general went to the king and asked if he should form together an army.

'Yes,' King Cronos said abruptly.

So an army of 11,000 set up and set off onto a march into the unknown. A little while went and the invasion force decided to rest at a small village called Terinala. All refreshed and restored the army marched on. It was what they thought, a clear run to the base but the enemy team appeared. There was a vicious battle which King Cronos won, just. Then they advanced and cut King Atihock's head off!

Jack Routledge (12)
Whitburn CE School, Whitburn

A Day In The Life Of Harry Potter

(Based on 'Harry Potter and the Philosopher's Stone' by J K Rowling)

Bang! The vase was thrown across the room at me.

'Are you happy, boy, now that you've ruined my new vase?' Aunt Petunia shrieked in my face, at the same time her spit going into my eyes. 'Well, are you, eh, eh?' as she still shrieked in my ear.

'Well . . . well it wasn't my fault now was it? I stammered.

'Don't take that attitude with your aunt; show her a bit of respect and not to mention me!' Uncle Vernon bellowed across the room.

I lowered my head, solemnly pretending to be ashamed of myself, but really I wasn't. After that I was sent to my cupboard under the stairs, moved along faster by a boot up the backside from the *wonderful* Uncle Vernon.

'Ow, that hurts!' I exclaimed, as I rubbed my behind at the same time.

'Well, you shouldn't be so slow when doing something then, should you?'

'Sorry,' I whispered sarcastically, as Uncle Vernon locked the cupboard door.

I lay on my bed in the darkness, then suddenly I heard a loud crashing noise. I opened the air vent on the old creaky door and saw a massive boot entering the doorway.

'Harry, Harry,' the man bellowed throughout the house, as the slates slid from the roof and hit the neighbours as they walked by.

'Hagrid, Hagrid, I'm in here,' I shouted as loudly as I possibly could. Hagrid put his hand on the doorknob and ripped the door off its hinges.

'Well, Harry you'd better get ready to go to Hogwarts, hadn't you? Chop, chop!'

Rae Lindstaedt (12)
Whitburn CE School, Whitburn

A Day In The Life Of Tomas Borqe

(Based on the poem 'Revenge' by Luis Enrique Mehia Godoy)

It's 1976, August 21st to be exact, and I am a prisoner. Imprisoned, what for? Murder, theft or illegal trade? No, simply for defending the rights of my people, the Nicaraguan people.

Alone I sit on the disgusting damp floor. In a hell which stinks of other men's sweat and tastes of humiliation. The drip, drip, drip of yesterday's rain slowly running off the rusty, corrugated roof above where I sit, adds to this mental torture. Outside I hear the monotonous conversation of my jailers and torturers in a language which I do not speak. And I crouch here like a captive tiger longing to be free.

I pray for the time when I can be the tiger running freely through the forest and not locked in a bare compound of a foreign zoo. I imagine the days when I can once again walk barefoot along the shore, hear the laughter of my children, watch the sun setting peacefully over the ocean. But I am not bitter; I will get my revenge.

My revenge, my personal revenge, will be to make you see the goodness in people's eyes, their dignity in victory, achieved by peaceful means. My revenge will be a haven where every brother and sister possess equal rights. Rights to education and liberation from our segregated quarter, so that we too can be part of the whole. When I see you, my jailer, I will not be afraid to greet you, 'Good morning', because I will no longer feel this bitterness. I will have had my revenge.

Katy Sutcliffe (16)
Whitburn CE School, Whitburn

A Day In The Life Of Grace Nichols

(Based on 'Abra-Cadabra' by Grace Nichols)

'You have more magic in your thumb than the length and breadth of any magician,' insisted my daughter, Faith, softly.

'I'm only doing my job Honey,' I replied comfortingly.

'No Mother. No you're not. All of my friends' mothers aren't nearly as magical as you are.'

I moved over to a small, dark cauldron in which I was preparing the dark green senna brew and said, 'I'm glad that you feel that way Faith but you don't understand that all mothers are magical to their own children.'

'No, Mother!' spoke Faith loudly. 'I do understand. I know enough to understand that you're the best mother in the whole wide world.' Faith fell silent.

I pulled an ancient wooden stool from beneath the bench, moved it over to the cauldron and sat down next to her.

I started weaving incredible stories of my youth; times when I would go to my friends' houses and stare in disbelief at some of the enchanting acts their mothers performed absolutely effortlessly.

As word after word streamed from my mouth the look on Faith's face was like a portrait of my youthful self: hanging onto her mother's words like an obedient dog hangs onto a stick.

My words halted suddenly as Faith's baby sister, Hope, hurried into the room shrieking that there was something up her nose. I took a crochet needle from the bench and gently tried to pry it out. Faith stood to my side like an inquisitive gaulding. She responded promptly as I ordered, 'Pass the black pepper.' Hope sneezed and the rest was history.

Jake Campbell (15)
Whitburn CE School, Whitburn

A Day In The Life Of Grandma Mariana

(Based on 'Grandma Mariana' by Alda do Espirito Santo)

I travelled from distant lands away from the bulls and the deaths, starting a new life, whether I liked it or not. I stand on the dusty ground outside the slave quarters smoking my gourd pipe, thinking of the times I was back in Cuba1. Times I'd rather forget about and times I miss. It seems like yesterday I was there, now washing away on the plantation is where I will stay. I remember clearly the journey on that sinister day.

The years are draining away, the continuous lifestyle I have, sitting on the dusty ground outside of the slave quarters in the blazing heat. I heard somebody cry out to me; 'Grandma Mariana, Grandma Mariana, it is time to leave.'

'I will stay here,' I replied.

An old woman like me has come to realise that I don't need to travel anymore. As lonely as I am, I am quite happy for this life to remain.

I sit at the doorstep of a dark alley, questions thrown at me by others; tell us your inglorious story. They wouldn't understand the life I've had. Continuing smoking, I sit; they don't understand why I won't tell about my past, the terrible life I led.

A young boy asks, 'Why did you cross the seas, and remain here all by yourself?'

'It was just something that I had to do, I am happy living this way.'

Elizabeth Plumpton (15)
Whitburn CE School, Whitburn

A Day In The Life Of Debjani Chatterjee

(Based on 'The Hungry Ghost' by Debjani Chatterjee)

Voices bombard me. The air is thick with clouds of spices. I am hallucinating in a world of colour. Suddenly, a hand, old and worn, grasps mine and keeps it held in its firm grasp. Safely.

The sunlight reaches through the open window. I open my eyes, encapsulated in a cocoon of coarse linen sheets. I knew that today I have to revisit that place. The place where I would float like a restless spirit, hungry for life.

The crystal sea is glistening, drenched in sunlight. The air is heavy, motionless. I hear the gentle rhythm of my father's footsteps next to mine. He is going to share my experience, visit the market with me.

We arrive at the market at mid-morning, to be greeted by the frantic buzzing of mopeds on the maze-like streets. So much has changed! The market seems to be bursting with goods, its bondage of buyers and sellers scurrying around the colourful stalls. Distances have shrunk but, alas, I have grown.

'Wanna buy a watch?' A man approaches us from a dark corner, his stall full of battered timepieces. We shake our heads in disbelief, amazed that the market has changed so much in such little time.

I miss the comforting hand of my grandfather, guiding through the crowds. I miss the spicy scents, the dense crowds, the market stalls brimming with fresh produce. I wish I was again that hungry ghost, watchful and floating through the world's noisy bazaar.

Philip Vasey (16)
Whitburn CE School, Whitburn

A Day In The Life Of Grandma Mariana

(Based on 'Grandma Mariana' by Alda do Espírito Santo)

Last night, I had a dream. The same dream I have every night. I was back in the land of vast plantations; the land I once called home. I was standing with no cares, no age and no chains. Without them I could run and jump: I could feel the wind interfering with my hair: but then, everything seems black again and the world stops. Suddenly I realise I'm still alone, even without the ties, even without the slavery, even without the daylight.

As I awoke, I looked around the cell I call my home and took a great sigh, thinking to myself the same thought I think every day. *Why did you cross the seas if this was to be your destiny?* Clambering out of bed, my feet were soon met by the cold floor, which made the struggle to stand that little more unbearable. Finally, the realisation that my youth has escaped me is taking its toll.

All I seem to do now is vegetate, in the shade of the yard, watching and admiring my grandchildren at the other side. Usually it is only five minutes before they ask me to tell stories of the past, and every day I refuse: today being no different. The memories of slavery; washing in this dark alley, washing my youth away; makes me sad and desperate. I do not wish to darken their souls along with mine.

Tomorrow will be no different; I know that much. Sitting here, on the back step, smoking my gourd pipe is all I was destined to do. So here I will stay, alone.

Miriam Phipps Bertram (16)
Whitburn CE School, Whitburn

A Day In The Life Of Harry Potter

(Based on 'Harry Potter and the Philosopher's Stone' by J K Rowling)

Monday morning, 7.25am. Looking around as I sit up on my bed, I am aware that most people are already up. I get up and put on my clothes. I walk down the stairs into the Gryffindor common room where Ron is sitting eating chocolates, while Hermione has her head in her book, like always. Hermione looks up at me, and then starts reading again. I walk over to the chair next to where Ron is sitting.

The head of Gryffindor house comes down the stairs saying, 'Everyone get up and get dressed, we have to be in the main hall in 5 minutes.'

Before I know it I am going downstairs and into the main hall where we all have our breakfast.

Just a lesson to follow - herbology with Professor Sprout. Followed by owl training with Hagrid.

I have a break now which is when I normally see Ron and Hermione. After break I have my flying lessons with Madam Hooch. I have my lunch now, normally outside with Ron.

I have a charms lesson with Professor Flitwick. After my boring lesson, I have an astronomy lesson with Professor Sinistra.

Now it is my free time but I have Quidditch practice for another hour. Then I go and play with friends. At 5 o'clock, everyone has to go to the main hall for our tea.

After tea it is dorm time where we stay in our dorms, and we play chess or study until 9.30 when the lights go out.

Kay Parmley (11)
Whitburn CE School, Whitburn

The Day And Life Of Harry Potter

(Based on 'Harry Potter and the Philosopher's Stone' by J K Rowling)

I found myself standing in the middle of King's Cross Station holding only a ticket and my luggage. The ticket that I was holding had written on it, 'King's Cross Station, platform 9¾, Hogwarts Express'.

I knew there wasn't such a thing as platform 9¾, so to be on the safe side I asked a station officer but he just walked away.

Suddenly I heard a family all with flaming red hair talking about 'Muggles', I knew by that they knew about platform 9¾. I started to follow the family. There were six all together.

We came up to platforms 9 and 10 but no platform 9¾, all that was there was a ticket booth. I stood and watched the family curiously as two twins ran with their older brother through the platform wall. I was stunned with amazement as the youngest brother was just about to run, until I had enough guts to ask how to get through. I walked over to the family and asked how to get through the platform wall. I stood up to run with Ron.

We ran and ran. I closed my eyes thinking I was going to crash but I didn't. I opened my eyes to find myself on a platform that wasn't there before. On a sign above my head there was writing on it saying 'Platform 9¾, Hogwarts Express'. And standing there without me noticing was a bright red train which had on it in bold lettering, 'The Hogwarts Express!'

Alexander Wood (11)
Whitburn CE School, Whitburn

A Day In The Life Of Harry Potter

(Based on 'Harry Potter and the Philosopher's Stone' by J K Rowling)

Hogwarts was the last place I would have expected to be going to when I started school in September. I woke up and threw off my blankets; I could smell the delicious bacon whiffing through the door.

I stood up and stumbled over one of Dudley's old toys, as I picked myself up I heard a rough voice shout up the stairs. It was Uncle Vernon.

'Hurry up Dudley and Harry, breakfast's ready.'

I whizzed around the room trying to find my clothes when I heard a bang then the sound of a herd of elephants running down the stairs.

'Harry hurry up,' Uncle Vernon bellowed.

'Coming,' I replied.

As I ran down the stairs I could taste the bacon in my mouth but I knew that I wasn't having that. There was a stale piece of bread in front of me.

'Hurry up, we need to get Dudley to the hospital.' Uncle Vernon picked up my trunk and put it in the boot of the car.

I got in the car and Uncle Vernon had to persuade Dudley to sit next to me. We drove for about fifteen minutes then we were there.

I was terrified by this point. Uncle Vernon put my trunk on the trolley and pushed it into the station. He seemed to be acting quite pleasant when we came to a sudden halt.

'They don't seem to have built the platform yet, do they?'

He was right, he gave a loud grunt. I was by myself.

Laura Dixon (12)
Whitburn CE School, Whitburn

A Day In The Life Of Harry Potter

(Based on 'Harry Potter and the Philosopher's Stone' by J K Rowling)

Bang, bang, bang.

I woke up as Dudley was jumping up and down on the stairs like a herd of elephants. As I got out of bed I banged my head on the ceiling of my tiny cupboard, it's under the stairs. As I opened the door Dudley slammed it shut in my face as he stormed past. When I walked into the kitchen, Aunt Petunia and Uncle Vernon stared at me and told me to fetch the post. I felt like saying, 'I'm not a dog, get Dudley to bring it.'

When I finally sat down to my breakfast, it turned out to be off milk from five days ago and two slices of toast that were burnt to a crisp, they were black. It was Dudley's birthday and it was time for him to open his presents.

'Thirty-six? Last year I had thirty-seven presents, that's one less than last year.'

'Yes, but some of your presents are a lot bigger than last year's.'

'I don't care how big they are, I want thirty-eight presents this year.'

'Well, we'll buy you two more presents when we are out today, OK?'

'I suppose so, can I open them now?'

'Of course, son.'

Aunt Petunia always gives in to him, she lets him do whatever he wants.

'Come on, Harry, we're waiting. Dudley and his friend are already in the car, chop, chop.'

'Just great, I'll be tortured by the time we arrive.'

Alice Urwin (12)
Whitburn CE School, Whitburn

A Day In The Life Of Harry Potter

(Based on 'Harry Potter and the Philosopher's Stone' by J K Rowling)

Bang, bang, bang. I suddenly woke up. I'd had the most amazing dream, that a man named Hagrid had come to take me to Hogwarts School. I would open my eyes to find myself in the cupboard with spiders on my quilt. But I opened my eyes to find Hagrid asleep on the sofa. But what was that banging noise?

At the window I saw a big black and white owl. I ran over and opened the window. It dropped the letters and swooped over and picked up Hagrid's coat.

''Arry will you give it three silver coins,' Hagrid grunted.

I snatched the coat of the owl and started raking through Hagrid's pockets. They were endless until I pulled 6 silver coins, they said 'Gringotts Bank'. Harry gave three of them to the owl. The owl flew out the window and I almost forgot about the letters until I saw them lying on the floor.

I picked them up and they told me what equipment I needed for school. It told me that I needed books, wands and uniform. It also told me that I could either bring a cat, owl or a toad.

'Hagrid I've got a letter about my equipment, but can we find all this in London?' I asked.

He said, 'Yes, if you know where to go.'

Anthony Jeffries (11)
Whitburn CE School, Whitburn

A Day In The Life Of Groundling

(Based on William Shakespeare and his theatre)

'It's busy today, I'm going to see Henry VIII, shall it be good or shall it be boring? That's the question to ask,' shouts Elizabeth. 'The tomatoes are already in my hand and I'm right up at the front if need be,' whispered Elizabeth quietly, as the actors walked on stage and started.

'The person sitting next to me is already asleep in the first five minutes, that's how boring it is, and I paid five pence to go and see this load of peevish mad-bred nut hook,' shouted Elizabeth.

'Right time to grab an ankle . . . *thump!* Yes right on his face,' shouted Elizabeth as loud as she could. 'There's a fight happening on the other side of the stage. Insults being thrown at each other, like thou rank, white-livered pantaloon and greasy lily-livered dogfish,' said Elizabeth in her normal voice. 'Argh! The police are here, better hide them tomatoes I stole,' whispered Elizabeth.

'Greetings Mary, how are you today?' says Elizabeth, in a happy way.

'I'm fine but this Henry VIII show is so boring, don't you think?' whispered Mary.

'Yes it is, however it gets me and you off the streets,' whispered Elizabeth back.

'Can I have some of your tomatoes please Elizabeth, I need to throw some at these rubbish actors?' asked Mary politely.

'You may have some tomatoes Mary, just make sure the police don't see them, I stole them the other day,' Elizabeth whispered very quietly.

'*Oh God!* I've hit the lantern and one of the curtains is on fire. *Run!*' shouted Mary as loud as she could.

Lindsey Miller (13)
Whitburn CE School, Whitburn

A Day In The Life Of Dejani Chatterjee

(Based on 'Hungry Ghost' by Dejani Chatterjee)

I walked with my father to the market; it reminded me of when I would follow my grandfather to the market. I felt I was back in time, women and children often followed behind men then.

The market is a noisy place, as I stepped into the market I was smacked in the face by the smell of spicy scents, India is popular for their spices.

I wondered around the stalls with my father absorbing the sights that surrounded me, a sea of movement and mingling. I have grown since my last visit, as has the market. However, it seems smaller, distances here have shrunk having travelled many places, changing my perception I once had as a child.

I have learned the value of money in this place now, for it is the bondage between buyers and sellers. I bought a lovely hat and some fresh fruit for lunch, however I almost wish I was that curious child like a hungry ghost again, watchful and floating through the noisy bazaar.

I left the bazaar with my father, taking the same route we came. The strong smell faded as the distance grew between us and the market. The voices washed away into the wind as we walked away. As I returned home I wondered when my next visit would be and how much more it will have changed.

Aaron Porter (16)
Whitburn CE School, Whitburn

A Day In The Life Of Freeman The Cane Cutter

(Based on 'The Four Knives of Freeman the Cane Cutter' by Ian McDonald)

Freeman the cane cutter spends most of his time in his home on the far side of the village, polishing his knives, for that is the reason he is famous in his village.

A curved knife, the one he spends the most time on, he keeps it clean and shiny. Rarely does it see the light of day, only when someone asks to see it or for a polish. $100 is the highest bid for this knife. Alas it was not enough in Freeman's eyes. But this is not the only one he praises.

The cane cutting knife that hangs above his bed at night like a Holy Cross, is also praised for it has been handed down from generation to generation of his fathers, the cane cutters. The shell handle at the end of the long blade, with its cut-bone sharpness is only used to cut the emerald ancestral fields. This knife is for working only, others, however, have other purposes.

The hard lime wood-handled knife has exquisite balance, this knife is his throwing knife. Cutting apples from the trees for a snack is this knife's main purpose, unless trouble is heading Freeman's way.

But his last one, the red-veined bone handle, used to slay the man who killed his wife, he keeps next to him at all times in memory of his ill-fated wife.

So Freeman sits at home in his humble solitude, polishing his prized knife, after a hard day's work in the cane fields.

Lee Forster (16)
Whitburn CE School, Whitburn

Young Writers – That's Write! Write Up Your Street Vol I

185

A Day In The Life Of A Groundling

(Based on William Shakespeare and his theatre)

Noise!

Today is a very special day. William Shakespeare is acting. Percy, our Irish actor, has fallen ill. There is nobody to take his place.

Slowly I walked up to the stage. With my bag on my shoulder, I was ready to distract the actors.

'Greetings my fellow man,' I muttered to an actor.

'Greetings,' he replied, 'thou saucy onion-eyed sniper.'

At that moment one of the most popular actors walked onto the stage; he had no idea what was in for him!

The show was starting. Me and my bag were ready and poised to start the throwing.

'To be or not to be? That is the question!' an actor exclaimed.

'Boo! Boo!' I shouted.

Now it's time to have some fun. An actor walked to the front of the stage with his arm firmly by his side. Clearly distracted by the hissing, he looked down and ground his teeth together at me.

Keeping my eyes fixed on him, I lowered my hand into my bag. I felt the foul, rotten plum I had been saving. Then with a smile on my face, I lowered my hand and my fingers wrapped round the plum. I raised it above my head and . . .

The roar of the crowd hit my ears.

'Throw, throw, throw!' they all chanted.

The actor's eyes opened wide. *Squelch!*

'Oh!' the crowd screamed.

Wiping his face he professionally carried on with the show. I thought that plum went to very good use; I was pleased that the crowd cheered and recognised my efforts.

A good day's work.

Owain Curtis (13)
Whitburn CE School, Whitburn

A Day In The Life Of A Groundling

(Based on William Shakespeare and his theatre)

'Greetings Mary, rubbish play. Is thou bored of that clay-brained actor too!' I exclaimed.

'Aye that be true,' agreed Mary, 'wish I was up there in the galleries,' she muttered.

'Thou would like so much to have a chair, only problem is you can't trip up the actor,' I remarked.

'Ow!' I shouted, felt my head and found a rotten plum. I thought, *this is it.* I pulled out the most rotten orange I could find and threw it at the actor on stage. I got him right in-between the eyes. He carried on acting.

'I hate this play, what is it called?' I demanded.

'I dunno, someone said it was called Mcbelty or sumfin,' she answered.

'I'm off to trip him up, he's rubbish isn't he?' I shouted.

'That he is,' agreed Mary.

I shoved my way to the front. I waited for the exact moment, then I yanked his legs and he smashed his head on the floor. He got back up and carried on, a little dazed by his fall.

'Thou rank paper face,' I shouted. I decided I should leave and thought, *what a waste of 1d.*

As I was leaving I saw a fight and I decided to join in. I jumped in and got hit straight back out into the wet, muddy floor. I was too old for punch-ups. I got up and looked up at the stage. A man was holding a skull in the air saying some sort of speech. I thought, *this isn't my sort of thing. I prefer comedies not boring tragedies.* I had been here for at least two hours and I was bored rigid. I picked up a mouldy fruit and threw it at the rank onion-eyed paper face. I don't know whether I hit him or not, so many other people were also throwing fruit and booing.

Satisfied, I shoved my way out of the theatre and went home.

David Blenkinsop (13)
Whitburn CE School, Whitburn

A Day In The Life Of Harry Potter

(Based on 'Harry Potter and the Philosopher's Stone' by J K Rowling)

Darker the night sky seemed to grow as my thoughts about the unusual three-headed dog raced through my mind. I had many thoughts. *Why was it there? Who did it belong to? Why did it have too many heads? Why was it so big?* and most of all, *what was the small wooden door under its huge paw?* All night I wondered about it but never worried. I knew I wasn't meant to be meddling in Hogwarts' business but I had to find out what it was doing there.

So the next morning I went to find Hagrid. When I found him I told him about it. He said it was his dog called Fluffy. He continued his story, recalling his conversation with a man in the pub saying that if you play music Fluffy will fall straight asleep. After telling me that he sounded nervous and whispered, 'I shouldn't have told you that.'

So I raced off grabbing Ron and Hermione by the arm. 'The dog is called Fluffy, it's guarding something and we're all in big trouble if we don't get there quickly, we have to beat him there.'

'Beat who?' said Ron.

'*Voldemort!*'

'What would Voldemort want with that thing?' replied Hermione.

'He's after what Fluffy is guarding and he knows how to put him to sleep. I think Fluffy is guarding the Philosopher's stone.'

Christopher Ovington (11)
Whitburn CE School, Whitburn

A Day In The Life Of Harry Potter

It was another dreary day in my cupboard. I spend half of my days here, the other half I spend doing tedious chores round the whole of the house and garden. This is how horrible the Dursleys are, by the way they're my aunt, uncle and cousin, they are the laziest people I know.

Bang, bang, bang! That will be Aunt Petunia.

'Hurry up, I want my tea, boy, and Dudley wants his toast!'

I'd better get up then, this day's chores will be on the kitchen table.

I get up and open the cupboard door. The sun blazes in my eyes. I rub them and go to the kitchen table. This day's chores: cook breakfast, mow the lawn, water the plants, tidy Dudley's room, cook tea, cook supper. This will keep me up till eleven o'clock at night!

'Get the post,' Uncle Vernon shouts from his seat at the table. 'We haven't got all day,' he growls from beneath his bushy moustache.

I grab the post and flick through it. One for Uncle Vernon, two for Aunt Petunia and what's this one for me? It even has my cupboard written on it. This is what it read: 'Mr H Potter, 4 Privet Drive, Little Whinging, Surrey, The Cupboard Under The Stairs'.

I walked into the kitchen reading the address over and over again, then, just as I was about to open it, Dudley snatched it right out of my hands.

Little did I know this was the letter that was going to change my life forever . . .

Siobhan Tedder (11)
Whitburn CE School, Whitburn

A Day In The Life Of Harry Potter

Eerily I was awoken by the faint noise of blankets above me. Unfortunately that didn't have an effect on the petrifying nightmares I was having about the horrifying day I survived - the killing of my parents. The beds of the dormitories were uncomfortable, they were like sleeping on the ground in winter, and the light was shining through the keyhole in the door making it hard for me to go to sleep. But I fell, once again, into a deep, deep, drowsy sleep.

Flash! Bang! Green and white flashes surrounded me, making me perplexed about what was happening, then there was a needle-sharp pain which I had never felt before, coming from my scar on my forehead. But this time it wasn't coming from the nightmare, it was real-life pain. Some foul magic was hitting me with so much force that I was blinded.

An evil force was attacking me. Little did I know the evil force killing me was the murderer of my parents. He was chanting, 'Die Potter, die'. Then there was a knock at the door. It was Dumbledore and Hagrid. There was a short time in my head of relief until I heard a loud tapping noise in my spine and I felt numb and useless. I felt nothing. Then I heard the soft voice of my mother which I had not heard in ages.

Joel Middleton (12)
Whitburn CE School, Whitburn

A Day In The Life Of Harry Potter

(Based on 'Harry Potter and the Philosopher's Stone' by J K Rowling)

I woke up one morning, excited to be going to Hogwarts. I got ready, packed my bags and sat there anxiously. I was waiting for Hagrid to arrive to take me to Hogwarts. He arrived, so I followed Hagrid to the train station and he gave me my ticket. It had on it Platform 9¾. I turned around and Hagrid had vanished.

I walked down the platform.

A lady said, 'Just run straight in the middle of platforms 9 and 10.'

I walked over to her and she asked me if I was going to Hogwarts. I said yes so she let me go in front of Ron. I ran at it and I was next to the Hogwarts Express. I saw Hagrid so I said hello to him. The train driver shouted, 'All aboard,' so I told Hagrid I'd see him at Hogwarts. I saw Ron so I sat down beside him and he showed me his rat. We stopped outside of Hogwarts and me and Ron felt anxious to get in.

We got in and Ron and me met a girl called Hermione. We walked into a gigantic dinner hall which had floating candles in mid-air. We walked up to the sorting hat and me, Ron and Hermione got put into Gryffindor. We went and sat down at our table and I don't know how but everyone knew my name. Hagrid was pleased for me, so was Professor Dumbledore.

Sam Prior (11)
Whitburn CE School, Whitburn